PRAISE FOR THE SHATTERING SEA

'A tremendous read... no end of dramas, surprises & reversals of fortune... a rattling good plot... wonderful stuff'
Fay Sampson, Guardian Children's Book Award-Nominated Author

'A born storyteller weaves Scottish island myths into a driving narrative of survival'
Ian Stephen, Saltire Award-Nominated Author

'I loved The Shattering Sea and devoured it in a single sitting. Urgent drama and ancient magic combine to make a wonderful story on the framework of an old, well-loved folk tale. Daniel Allison has the storyteller's gift of linking compelling narrative with lively, poetic prose. An exciting debut.'
Peter Snow, Author of A Rosslyn Treasury and The Shifty Lad

PRAISE FOR FINN & THE FIANNA

'A masterpiece... this is Celtic myths and legends at their fantastic best! Your eyes dare not blink for fear of missing a single word. Mythical, flirty, thumpingly violent and divinely nasty!'

Jess Smith, Author of *Way of the Wanderers*

FREE DOWNLOAD OFFER

As the winter winds shriek and their family sleeps, Grunna and Talorc sit at the hearth-fire, telling the tales of Ancient Orka. Stories of trowies, silkies and even the mysterious Silvers.

I'm offering *Silverborn* as a FREE ebook exclusively to members of the House of Legends Clan. Visit my website to collect and download. It's fast, free and easy.

Get my FREE ebook at www.houseoflegends.me/landing-page

CONTENTS

Introduction   xiii

1. The Cailleach   1
2. The Tale Of The Hoodie   6
3. Tam Lin   21
4. Orangey & Appley   31
5. Death In A Nut   40
6. The Battle of the Birds   48
7. Fox & Dog   81
8. The Silkie Wife   87
9. The Well at World's End   98
10. A Close Tongue   109
11. Lady Odivere   119
12. Taming the Kelpie   136
13. The Fairy Lover   144
14. The Makers of Dreams   153
15. The Cattle of Pabbay   161
16. The King & The Cockerel   166
17. Asipattle and the Stoor Worm   172
18. The Well of Youth   182
19. The Mermaid Bride   188
20. The Seal Hunter   201
21. The House of Riddles   209
22. The Knight of the Red Shield   216
23. The King of Norway's Brown Horse   229
24. The Snake Shirt   253
    Author's Note   281
    Free Download Offer   285
    The Shattering Sea (Sample Chapter)   286

The Shattering Sea: Book I of The Orkney   291
Cycle
Finn & The Fianna   293
Recommended Reading   295
House of Legends Podcast   297
Storytelling Coaching   299
Book Coaching   300

Acknowledgments   301
About the Author   303

In loving memory of Peter Lewis, the best man I ever knew.

INTRODUCTION

There is a Scottish folk tale named *Donald Din*. The hero of the story has a dream in which he travels to London and finds treasure. He duly sets off for London, but finds no treasure.

Standing on London Bridge, Donald meets a man who once dreamed of finding treasure in a cabbage patch in Argyll. Donald realises that the stranger is talking about Donald's own cabbage patch. He returns home and digs up the treasure that is rightly his.

This story is found in different guises all over the world. It was made into a novel, *The Alchemist*, which has sold over 65 million copies. Why? Because so many of us are like Donald.

I grew up in Scotland knowing nothing of Scottish myths and legends. As far as I knew, we didn't have any. At school, myths and legends meant Greek myths and legends. I loved those stories, and read them over and over again. Perhaps if I had been a bit brighter, I might have asked my teachers if we had any stories of our own.

I don't know what the answer would have been. British people tend to believe that culture came with the Romans and left with the Romans. The 'What did the Romans ever do for us?' joke from Monty Python is repeated often, as if it confirms that we had nothing before we had running water and wine.

We did, of course, have our own cultures and our own stories. I discovered these stories as an adult, when I took up oral storytelling and finally did some digging beneath my own cabbage patch. Like Donald Din, I found treasure.

Scotland's stories are unlike the Greek and Norse myths you're probably familiar with. The primary difference is that almost none of our stories speak of gods. While the ancient people of Scotland undoubtedly had their gods, most have not survived in the stories handed down to us; not overtly, anyway.

As in so many places, the early Christians sought to displace the old religions in Scotland. On the face of it, they succeeded. But our gods might not have been driven out entirely. They may have gone underground, burrowing from myth into legend, hiding beneath the surface like the treasure under Donald's cabbage patch.

Thus, we have the legends of the Fianna. Finn MacCoull

and his warriors were once known to everyone across the Gaelic-speaking world. They were responsible for forging prominent features of the landscape, such as the Giant's Causeway in Ireland. We have the trickster-hero Asipattle, who fights a gigantic serpent and is responsible for the making of Orkney, Shetland and Faroe. It seems to me that the old gods of Scotland lurk behind Finn and Asipattle.

Scotland's stories strike an incredible variety of tones. There are humorous stories, tragedies and quests; we meet Viking lords, seal-people and ferrymen; we glimpse ancient magical rituals.

One reason for this is the incredible variety of Scotland's landscapes, from the rugged mountains of the highlands to the pastures of the Borders. These landscapes are not just backdrops; they are the lifeblood of stories. While some stories happily flit from place to place, putting down roots as they go, others are very specific to their locale. Stories featuring the finmen are unique to Orkney and Shetland, and may recall voyages made by Saami from Finland. The hallucinatory legends of the highlands are part of a Gaelic culture that never existed in Southern Scotland.

To read, hear or tell these stories connects us to the ancient past and a living tradition. After centuries on the fringes, the role of the storyteller was taken up in recent decades by people such as Donald Smith, Ruth Kirkpatrick and David Campbell, who learnt the art from Travellers such as Duncan Williamson, Sheila Stewart and Stanley Robertson. The Scottish Storytelling Centre has been established on Edinburgh's Royal Mile, home to the world's only purpose-built storytelling theatre. A new generations of tellers has taken up the art there, so that once again, storytelling in Scotland is flourishing.

Duncan Williamson used to say, 'Stories were our education'. You can't reduce such complex creatures as these stories to a moral, but they have plenty to teach us. The hoodie's wife teaches tenacity as she sits by the blacksmith's fire, sweat pouring down her as she pumps the bellows. Asipattle knowns when it's time to lie still, like a sleeping wildcat, before leaping into action.

Tune your ear to the dream-speak of stories. We need them, now more than ever.

1

THE CAILLEACH

Darkness.

Silence.

A time before time.

In that time, the Cailleach came.

She came from the North, from further north than North, atop a throne of storms. Blue-skinned and white-eyed, her breath so cold that it shattered stars, the Cailleach sought a new home.

Beneath her, she spied a mass of rock. It had no shape; no peaks nor valleys, no trees nor rivers, no birds nor four-footed things.

It had no gods.

The rock called to her. She sang to it, and it roared at her. *Make a home here*, it said. *Sink your hands into me. Make me anew.*

The Old Woman of Winter was pleased. She landed on the rocks, making the whole world shake.

Amid swirling storms, the Cailleach set to work.

The Crone plunged her hands into the eager rock. Grinding and breaking and pummelling the stone, she forged it anew.

The Cailleach made mountains. Armies of mountains. Legions of mountains. A stone forest of bristling teeth; a galaxy of temples to snow, cold and screaming wind. The wind swirled around her, urging her on, cladding her creation in icy armour.

After time uncounted, the Cailleach looked about herself. She was nearly finished. All she needed was a seat from which to observe her home. With the last of her strength, she built a shoreside mountain that towered above all the others. Finally, she climbed atop it and lay down to sleep.

The Cailleach was thirsty when she awoke. She climbed down from her seat and wandered among the mountains until she found one pregnant with pure water.

With her bare hands, she cut a hole in its side. The Cailleach lifted out the stopper of stone she had made, set it aside and put her mouth to the mountain, sucking at its nectar. The water enlivened her. She decided to go wandering and get a few things done.

The Cailleach noticed that the white plaid she wore was dirty. She walked out into the sea and washed it in the water. The water still whirls in that place, sucking unwary sailors into the sea. When her plaid was clean, she lay it out over the mountains to dry. She still does this today; her plaid appears to us as a mantle of snow upon the mountaintops.

The Cailleach had recovered from her great labour. She roved her rocky home every day and drank from her mountain spring every night. One night, she forget to replace the stopper. All night, water poured from the mountain and filled the glens from east to west. So Scotland's web of lochs and rivers was made.

Life was quickening.

As the Cailleach slept upon her throne, she dreamed of a being absolutely unlike her. A maiden, golden-haired and with sun-kissed skin, danced upon a loch shore. Beneath her bare feet bloomed snowdrops and violets, foxgloves and daffodils.

The Cailleach dreamed of Bride, Maiden Of Summer.

When the Cailleach awoke, she saw to her horror that green grass had broken the ice in the valleys. Summer birds were everywhere, singing in praise of Bride.

The Cailleach took her holly wand and brought it crashing down on the landscape. Ice shot outwards from it in every direction, cloaking the land in winter again.

Yet still, the Cailleach dreamed of summer.

When she next awoke, she felt her face. It was smoothing out; her wrinkles were disappearing. Strands of gold shone in her hair.

The Cailleach howled in fury. She screamed songs of winter, summoning storms from the far North that ground mountains into dust. Yet in her heart, Bride laughed and sang.

This went on until, one day, the sun rose over the Seat of the Crone. It rose, not on the Cailleach, but on Bride.

So began the first day of spring.

Bride danced down from the mountaintop, twirling and laughing. She danced from North to South and from East to West, life bursting into being all around her. Roaring stags raised their antlers to the sun; bears fished for salmon by the silvery rivers. Butterflies and bees mirrored Bride in their shimmering wings.

Life rejoiced in its rapturous unfolding. Then, in time, Bride's song slowed. It grew gentler.

Gold glimmered in the fading forests. Bride surrendered to dreams of silence, sharp starlight and brittle earth.

On the last day of autumn, Bride fell asleep. On the first day of winter, the Cailleach awoke. She wore her white shroud of winter, yet summer slept in her heart. [1]

---

1. *Stories about the Cailleach are found all over Scotland and Ireland. This version of her tale was inspired by a few sources, including a stage performance by David Campbell and Janis Mackay.*

   In Ireland, the Cailleach is also known as Beera. There is a beautiful area of Ireland called the Beera Peninsula which is named after her; do visit if you ever get the chance.

   In Glean Cailliche, a glen in the heart of Scotland, a tiny hut is home to stone figurines of the Cailleach and her family. Local shepherds put the figures in or out of the hut on the first day of spring and winter. Some believe this to be Britain's oldest surviving pagan ritual.

2

THE TALE OF THE HOODIE

There once lived in the west a farmer and his three daughters. They kept cattle and goats, grew barley and wheat and harvested kelp from the shore. The sisters argued over everything they could think to argue over, but when times were tough they pulled together.

One crisp autumn day, the sisters walked to the river to wash their clothes. The two eldest sisters worked side by side beneath a beech tree, singing songs in harmony as they worked. The youngest sister went to work a little way down-river, as she fancied being alone with her thoughts.

As the elder sisters worked and the wind tussled the grass, they heard the cry of a hoodie crow. A moment later, the hoodie landed on a branch of the beech, tucked in its black wings and called to the eldest sister.

'Young beauty,' he said. 'I have flown far in search of a wife. If you will have me, I will take you as my wife.'

'You must be joking!' said the eldest sister. 'I would sooner leap off the edge of the world than marry a hideous hoodie.'

The hoodie didn't look the least bit troubled by this. He turned to the second sister and said, 'Young beauty. I have flown far in search of a wife. If you will have me, I will take you as my wife.'

'The day I marry you will be the day a cow marries a frog,' said the second sister.

The two of them laughed as the hoodie flapped its wings and flew away.

Nearby, the youngest sister was adrift in the river of her thoughts when she heard a whooshing of wings. The hoodie flew down and landed on the grass beside her, close enough that she could have reached out and stroked him.

'Young beauty,' it said. 'I have flown far in search of a wife. If you will have me, I will take you as my wife.'

The girl put aside her washing and gave the hoodie her full attention.

'Will you treat me kindly?' she asked.

'I may sometimes be angry, but I shall never be cruel,' he said.

'Will you amuse me?'

'You will be sad at times, but you will never be bored.'

'Will you always be a hoodie?'

'It is up to you. I can be a hoodie by day and a man by night, or a man by day and a hoodie by night.'

'I would rather you be a hoodie by night, when I am asleep. Very well; I will marry you.'

They promised themselves to another. Once the words that made them man and wife had been spoken, the girl said goodbye to her sisters, and to her father, who was back at the house.

Returning to her husband, she saw that he had grown large enough to carry her on his back. She clutched the feathers of his neck between her hands, and they flew away.

Over the glens and through a forest of mountain peaks they flew, heading due north. They flew all night, and by the sun's first light they reached the hoodie's home, a towering fortress clad in black feathers.

The hoodie became a man, handsome and elegant. He and his wife ate and drank together, celebrating their marriage. That night, as the girl fell asleep in her husband's arms, he became a hoodie and flew out into the darkness.

Time passed. The girl grew pregnant and in time gave birth to a son. His father cradled the boy in his arms and spoke blessings over him.

That night, after the hoodie flew away, his wife was lying in bed with her babe in her arms when she heard music. It was being played on an instrument she had never heard before. She closed her eyes, enraptured by the delicate, beautiful notes, and when she next opened them, it was morning.

Sunlight streamed in through the window of her bedchamber.

Her child was gone.

She ran from room to room, calling and then screaming for her son, but he was nowhere to be found. Her husband returned home and was as dismayed as she was. They searched in vain for their son, and wept until they had no more tears.

At length, the girl grew pregnant again. She gave birth to another son on a bright spring morning; that night, she determined to stay awake until dawn.

Her husband became a hoodie and left her. Deep in the night, his wife heard that same music. When she awoke, her child was gone.

Even deeper was their grief this time. The girl howled like a tortured wolf; her husband spoke curses that darkened the sky.

For a third time, the girl became pregnant.

A son was born to her in autumn. His parents held him tightly all day, barely blinking as they gazed at him, praying that the night would not come. It came as it must, and the husband became a hoodie and flew outside.

Once more, his bride lay awake, nursing her son.

The hours passed.

Night's darkest hour arrived.

Brilliant music stole through the air. The hoodie's wife wailed and cursed, pinching and biting herself in a desperate effort to stay awake.

She fell asleep. In the morning, she awoke alone.

Her husband, a man once more, entered their bedchamber.

Their eyes met. She saw a shadow fall within him, as if the hundred fires that burned in his heart had gone out.

'Get dressed,' he said, before turning and leaving.

The hoodie's wife dressed, went downstairs and found the door to the fortress open. Outside was a black carriage attached to a team of horses. Her husband was waiting inside the carriage.

'We are going away for a while. Do you have everything you need for a journey?' he asked her as she climbed inside.

'Yes.'

The horses at once began to move. The carriage passed out of the gates and took a road leading into the forest.

After they had left the fortress far behind, the girl put her hand in her pocket.

'I have forgotten my comb,' she said. 'Can we go back, or–'

Her husband cried out as if in pain. The carriage became a withered stick of wood; the horses disappeared. She fell to the ground, landing hard, as her husband became a hoodie crow again. He flew around her three times, cawing furiously, and flew away.

'Come back!' she called as her husband became a dot in the sky. He didn't come back. He grew smaller and smaller until he vanished into the distance.

'He'll come back to me,' she told herself. 'He'll come back.'

But she knew it wasn't true. He wasn't coming back.

She got to her feet and dusted herself off. Casting around, she found a stick of hazel wood to use as a staff.

'If he will not come back to me,' she said, 'then I shall find him.'

The hoodie's wife set off through the forest, in the direction her husband had flown.

All day she walked. She had given birth only the day before, and walking was a great labour for her. Yet she kept on going, down winding woodland paths and through boggy moors, up onto the wind-scoured hills. Whenever she reached a hilltop or mountain peak, she would see the dark shape of her husband in the next glen; and when she reached the glen, she would see him atop the next hill.

This went on all day. When the day darkened, she found herself on the shore of a loch. Not far down the shore she saw a house, light gleaming in its windows. She went to the house and saw a woman standing in the doorway.

'Come in,' said the woman, 'and pass the night.'

Inside, a fire was burning in the hearth and a pot of stew was cooking over the fire. Playing on the rug before the fire was a little boy.

The girl sat down at the table and gratefully accepted a bowl of stew. As she ate, she watched the boy. He was playing with a little man woven from straw. The boy laughed and smiled as he played, and she felt as if her heart was being pressed between two stones.

'What business are you about?' asked the woman.

'I am chasing my husband,' said the girl, 'a hoodie crow.'

'Rest here tonight,' said the woman, 'and stay your path tomorrow. Your husband passed by here today, and if you follow him, you shall catch up with him.'

The girl slept on the rug in front of the fire. In the morning, she left the house. She skirted the loch and climbed the next hill, and from there she spied her husband in the next glen. The day went the same way as the previous day, and by evening her feet were blistered and every muscle in her body ached terribly. Still, she went on.

In the evening, she spied the light of a house. It looked a long way off through the trees, but in no time at all she reached it. The woman of the house welcomed her in, sat her down and fed her bread and broth.

'You'll be searching for your husband,' said the woman.

'He was here only a little while ago. Keep on going and you'll find him.'

The girl nodded and thanked the woman, her eyes on a little boy who played in front of the fire, juggling balls of cloth. She wished she could hold him, stroke his hair and sing to him.

Night passed, morning came and the girl set out once more. She spied her husband swooping over the next hill. With new speed and strength, she set off after him. She ignored the pain in her feet and everywhere else, listening for his cries that cut the cold air. Yet try as she might, she could not catch up to him. When dusk bit the day, she was forced to stop again.

Spying the light of a house, she went that way. The woman of the house ushered her in.

Sat by the fire, singing to himself, was a young boy.

The woman of the house filled a bowl with broth and gave it to the girl. She gulped it down, for she was desperately hungry, and the woman gave her another.

'I'm looking for–'

'Your husband,' said the woman. 'And you shall find him. He was here just before you. For now, you need your bed.' The woman took her empty bowl, and she lay down to sleep by the fire.

In the night she awoke.

Someone was there beside her. She could hear their breathing.

Whoever it was slid a ring onto her finger.

She opened her eyes and saw who it was.

Her husband.

As soon as her eyes met his in the ember-light, he turned and flew for the open door.

'No! Come back!' she cried as she tried to grab him and pull him down. She only succeeded in pulling out one of his feathers.

It was many hours later when she fell asleep again, clutching the inky feather. When she awoke it was still dark outside, her breath steaming in the firelight.

The woman of the house was awake. She brewed tea for the girl and sat down opposite her on the rug.

'You will find your husband,' she said. 'But you will not find him today, nor the next day. He has crossed the Hill of Poison. I heard of a man who crossed it once, but that was in the time when ivy grew on the stars. If you wish to cross it, you will need to wear horseshoes on your hands and feet, and you must forge them yourself.'

The girl listened as the woman gave her directions to the nearest village. They said goodbye, and the girl went out into the frosty dawn. The road led her to a wider road, which led to a village. She found the smithy and knocked on the door.

It turned out that the blacksmith was in need of an assistant. She took the job and set to work immediately, sweating as she worked the bellows all day before collapsing asleep upon the forge-floor at night.

She was a hard worker, and the smith grew fond of her. He took pleasure in teaching her the secrets of his craft. When she asked him if she might make some horseshoes to keep for herself, he said, 'Of course you may.'

The winter passed. Come spring, she was strong and lean. She had learned her craft well and forged four perfect shoes for herself.

It was time to leave.

The hoodie's wife thanked the smith and said goodbye. Out of the village and back into the wilds she went, crossing lonely glens until she stood at the foot of the Hill of Poison.

Thick, black, bubbling liquid covered the ground. Not a bush or tree or blade of grass grew anywhere. The acrid smell made her head spin, but she didn't hesitate. She lay down her staff, took the shoes from her pack and strapped them to her boots and hands.

Carefully, she placed her left hand upon the poison-soaked ground. The poison hissed. She set down her right hand and began to climb.

Up and up she went, her arms trembling, her shoulders screaming. The strength she had gained in the forge saw her through. At last, in the dim light of the winter noon, she reached the top and looked down over the far side of the hill.

There was a village in the glen. She spied a market square, clusters of little houses and a great, grand house behind walls and gates.

Downhill she went, loping like a wolf, her body full of new strength. Before long she was at the foot of the hill, where she unstrapped her horseshoes and went back to walking on two legs. It felt strange after a day on all fours.

She entered the village and wandered through the marketplace. The folk there were strange. Some had eyes on the ends of their fingers, while others had the heads and tails of wild creatures. At one market stall, men paid to be spat on and cursed by an old woman. A finely-dressed cat strolled along, leading a tiny man on a leash.

The girl had a few copper coins, and she used them to buy a mug of tea. While drinking her tea, she fell to talking with a plump, four-armed woman, and asked her for the news.

'You'll not be from around here, if you don't know the news,' said the woman. 'The Lord's daughter is getting married tonight, to a stranger from over the hill. There'll be dancing in the streets, but I shall miss it all, for I'm a cook in the Lord's kitchen. I'll be busy cooking the wedding supper.'

'That's a shame,' said the girl. 'How about I take your place? I can cook, and I don't mind missing the dancing.'

'Well, if you're sure,' said the cook.

'I'm sure,' said the girl. The cook thanked her, and she headed off in the direction of the Lord's house.

She found the kitchens and got to work. Just as she finished the soup, a butler called that the wedding party were ready to eat.

'Is the soup ready?' he asked.

'It is,' she said.

Before she stepped back from the pot, she slipped into it two things. One was the ring from her finger, that the hoodie had placed upon it as she slept. The other was the feather she had pulled from his back.

Upstairs, surrounded by candles, silver and people of high station, her husband sat beside his new bride.

She smiled at him, held his hand and spoke with sparkling wit. He laughed, sipped his whisky and wondered why he felt so out of sorts. This was his wedding day, and he was marrying the Lord's daughter; shouldn't he be feeling happy?

Since flying over the Hill of Poison, riven with grief for his stolen sons, the hoodie had forgotten who he was. Of his first wife, his fortress and his stolen sons, he remembered not a thing. He knew something was wrong, though. It was as if he had an itch but couldn't figure out where.

'Ah, the soup!' said his bride. 'Cook does make such wonderful soup.'

Smartly-dressed servants appeared before them and

filled their bowls with hot, steaming soup. He was just dipping his spoon into his bowl when he noticed something odd.

There was a feather in his soup.

He fished it out with his spoon. As he did so, something else floated to the surface.

A ring.

He set the feather down on the table. Lifting the ring from his spoon, he wiped it on his shirtsleeve and traced its shape with his fingers.

He turned to the waiter, who was eyeing him nervously.

'Bring me the one who made this soup,' he said.

Images tugged at the edge of his memory. A black-feathered castle, a child...

In came the four-armed cook, who had slipped back into the kitchens after enjoying the dancing.

'Is there something the matter with the soup, my Lord?' she asked him.

He stared at her.

'Not you,' he said. 'You didn't make this soup. Bring me the one who made it.'

Red-faced, she scurried from the room and down the stairs.

He waited, fingering the ring and the feather. His bride tried in vain to get his attention, but he wouldn't listen.

Footsteps sounded on the stairs.

Into the room walked a woman he had never seen before. Only... he had seen her.

He knew her.

The bridegroom stood.

'I cannot marry,' he said. 'For this woman is my wife.'

The Lord, the Lord's daughter and all their guests cried out in consternation. They pounded their fists on the tables and threw their drinks over the pair. Grabbing his wife's hand, the bridegroom ran from the room, down the stairs, out the door and out the gates. They didn't stop running until they reached the Hill of Poison.

'We must cross quickly,' he said. 'They will be after us.' Sure enough, they could hear stamping and snarling and shouting; the sounds of pursuit.

The wife took her iron shoes from her pack and strapped them to her hands and boots. 'I will go first,' she said, 'and I will throw the shoes back to you as I walk.'

She began climbing. After each step she took, she unstrapped and threw one of her shoes back to him, so he could take a step; he would take a step then throw the shoe back to her. The shoes flew back and forth between them, and when their pursuers arrived at the foot of the hill, they were too far up it to catch.

It was slow work, but they made it up and over the hill, and finally reached the other side. They stowed the shoes in her pack and kissed, their kiss full of fierce love.

That night, they slept in the third house where the girl

had stopped. This woman, it turned out, was the sister of the hoodie. The boy who had sat telling stories by the fire was their son. The boy, his mother and his father held one another, laughed and wept.

On the next night, they visited the second house where the girl had stopped. She was also a sister of the hoodie. The boy who had juggled balls by the fire was their second stolen son. They juggled and played with him far into the night.

The final night of their journey was spent at the first house where the girl had stopped. The woman there was, of course, the hoodie's sister, and the boy with the straw doll was their first stolen son.

In the morning, the whole family departed together. They made their way up and down mountain paths until they reached their home. I visit them often, and all is well there. [1]

---

1. *I found this story in J.F Campbell's* Popular Tales of the West Highlands. *It isn't a particularly well-known story, and I've never heard another storyteller tell it. Other stories similar to it are very popular, however. The most prominent are* East Of The Sun, West Of The Moon, *from Scandinavia, and* Eros & Psyche. East Of The Sun, West Of The Moon *was made into a film in the 1980's, but the production company lost funding while making it, so the film was cancelled.*

Crows are closely associated in Celtic mythology with the Morrigan, a goddess of battle. If you're interested in the symbology of the crow, The Tain Bo Cuailgne *should be at the top of your list.*

3

TAM LIN

Nestled within the hills of the Scottish borders is a place called Carterhaugh. If you go there, you will see fields, woods, cottages and a farmhouse. There is nothing to suggest that something extraordinary once happened there. But it did.

In days gone by, the Lord of Carterhaugh lived in that farmhouse. He owned all the land that could be seen in every direction, and he had a daughter named Janet.

One summer's day, when her father wasn't at home, Janet stood by her window, gazing out over their lands. She was bored. Janet never had any chores to do, as servants did all the housework, and she had no friends living nearby for company.

As she stood there, her thoughts circling like buzzards,

the sun shone through the clouds and lit up a woodland at the far end of the glen.

'I have lived here all my life,' said Janet to herself, 'yet for some reason, I have never walked in those woods.'

She smiled. For once, she had something to do. She would go and explore those woods.

Downstairs she went. She rung for the maid and said she was going for a walk. The maid fetched her coat and asked Janet where she would go walking.

'Oh no,' said the maid when she heard Janet's answer. 'You mustn't go walking there, Miss.'

'Why not?' asked Janet.

The maid looked distinctly uncomfortable. 'Well, Miss, they say a fairy man lives in those woods. Tam Lin is his name, and they say that whenever a maiden walks in those woods, he takes something from her. Gold, or silver, or... her decency.'

'Well, I'm sure I won't see any fairy man,' said Janet, 'and if I do, he certainly won't be taking anything from me.'

The maid tutted and shook her head, but Janet went on her way.

Down the road walked Janet. She came to the woods and found a path leading beneath the leaves.

The path was wide, the woods quiet. Janet strolled along

with a smile on her face. It felt good to be out of the house, good to be among the trees and good to do something that was perhaps a little dangerous. She didn't believe there was a fairy man in the woods, but the idea made an ordinary walk far more interesting.

Janet walked beneath ash and hazel and oak trees, beside little winding streams and a spidery old yew, its branches planted in the soft, loamy earth. At length she came to a cross in the road with an ancient, crumbling well beside it. Her maid had told her about this place; it was called Miles Cross.

Looking around, Janet spied a rose at the side of the road.

Her heart skipped a beat. Could it be?

She ran over and knelt down. It was a two-headed rose! Janet loved herbs and flowers of all kinds, and she had never seen a two-headed rose before. She would pluck it, take it home and plant it in her garden.

Janet reached out to pluck it; then she paused. This was a strange wood. It might be better to leave it as it was.

She plucked it anyway.

The moment she did so, she shrieked and dropped the rose; for a man appeared out of nowhere in front of her.

She stared at him. He smiled at her. His lips were red, his mouth was small and his dark hair fell in shining curls over his shoulders. His smile somehow made him look both pleased and angry.

'That flower was not yours to pluck,' he said.

'These woods are not yours, to tell me what I can and cannot do,' said Janet.

'Oh, but they are,' said the man, who was surely Tam Lin. 'Whatever any piece of parchment might say, these woods are mine. I am these woods, and these woods are me.'

'Nonsense,' said Janet.

'You shall see,' said Tam.

Janet blinked, and Tam was gone.

Janet had no appetite to remain in those woods. She turned and walked back the way she came. Reaching the edge of the woods, she left the shelter of the trees and rejoined the main road.

The sun was blindingly bright. It hurt her head. She slowed her steps, her feet feeling heavy.

'I must be coming down with something,' she told herself. 'I'll go to bed and rest when I get home.'

Finally, she reached her father's house. There were a number of carriages outside; evidently her father had returned and brought guests. She didn't want to see anyone; she would go straight upstairs to her room. Oh, she felt awful.

Janet opened the front door. She slipped through and tried to close it quietly, yet it banged shut. The hallway seemed to be spinning.

'Janet? Janet, come in here a moment,' called her father.

She sighed and entered the drawing room. The Lord of Carterhaugh sat there surrounded by lords, ladies and well-to-do merchants.

They were all staring at her.

'Janet? Janet... what on earth has happened to you?' asked her father.

'I've been for a walk,' she said, annoyed at his idiotic question.

'Good lord!' said one of the ladies. 'She's pregnant!'

'Pregnant? Don't be ridiculous!' said Janet. Yet when she looked down, she saw that her stomach had ballooned. She did feel awfully heavy...

'She must have been to the woods. This will be Tam Lin's work,' said someone. 'Foolish girl.'

Janet looked up. It was that dreadful young lord from Duns who had tried to court her.

'Foolish girl?' she said, the room spinning around her. 'I'll tell you who is foolish. You are! You are jealous that I am pregnant by Tam Lin and not you, you lecherous oaf.'

Without stopping to listen to another word, she turned and left the room. Back out the front door she went, headed for Tam Lin's wood.

The next time Janet saw Tam Lin, it was his feet she saw. She didn't bother to look up.

'What are you doing?' he asked.

'Looking for medicine to cure my condition,' she said.

'No!'

Janet stood up, one hand on her belly. 'No? Tell me why I should not.'

'Because of my love for you.'

'Your love,' said Janet. 'Tam Lin, you have met me once. You are a fairy. Your kind and my kind are not–'

'I'm not a fairy,' he said.

Janet rolled her eyes.

'I'm not a fairy, Janet,' said Tam. 'I'm a mortal man. I once lived with my family, in a house not far from where your house stands now. Even in those days, folk warned others against walking in these woods. It was not me they warned of, back then; it was the Queen of the Fairies.

'I was riding through these woods, near this very spot, when a man appeared on the road in front of me. My horse reared up, and I was thrown from his back and caught by her. By the Fairy Queen.

'She took me through soil and stone, to her hall beneath the hill. There I have lived as her servant, and there I thought I would remain until the sun ceases to rise. But I have fallen out of favour, and soon I will no longer be hers.'

'Why not?' asked Janet.

'Every year, our Queen pays a tithe to Hell. I have been

chosen this year. Tonight she will ride out from her hall, across the country to the Gates of Hell, and hand me over. That is, unless you help me. If you save me, I will not belong to Hell, nor to her. I will belong to myself, and you.'

'If I were to help you,' said Janet, 'what would I have to do?'

'Return here at midnight,' said Tam. 'Wait at the side of the road.

'You will hear the beating of hooves,' he went on. 'Three horses will gallop by. Ignore the first and the second. Look to the third, a white mare. I will be upon it. You must seize me and pull me down.

'When you pull me to the ground, my form will change. I will become a beast, and then a beast of another kind, and then another. Through all my changes, you must hold me tightly. You won't be hurt. Don't let go until I become a burning coal. At that point, throw me into the well. I shall become a man once more, naked and unbound.'

'I am not saying I love you,' said Janet. 'But I will not let you pass through the Gates of Hell. I will return tonight.'

As the stars shone down on Carterhaugh, Janet hid among the bushes by Miles Cross.

But for the screeching of an owl, all was silent. Janet stroked her belly and tried to calm her fears. All she had to do was pull Tam Lin from the horse, hold him tightly and throw him into the well. It should be simple enough.

She was beginning to think that nothing would happen when she heard hoofbeats on the road.

Janet got to her feet. She crept to the very edge of the road, peering around the trunk of an oak. The hoofbeats grew louder and louder.

She spied the horses.

The first, a black, came racing past. A grey horse followed it. Behind the grey was a white mare.

Tam sat atop it.

Janet ran at the horse. She grabbed Tam's ankle, wrenched his foot free of the stirrup and pulled him to the ground.

Tam collapsed on top of her. His yell became a hiss as he became a cold-skinned adder, writhing and biting as he tried to evade her.

Janet shrieked in pain as he bit her, but held on.

Tam became a swan. His beak struck at her; his wings flapped furiously.

Janet clung on.

Tam became a bear, so huge that he could have torn her in two. His roar was deafening. He grasped her so tightly that she though her bones would be crushed. Despite her terror and pain, Janet clung on.

Tam became a lion. She screamed into his mane as he sunk his teeth into her shoulder, clawing at her back.

He can't harm me, Janet told herself. *He won't harm me.*

Tam was no longer a lion. He became a red hot coal and fell to the forest floor.

With a roar of her own, Janet grabbed the coal and flung it into the well.

The water of the well hissed, steamed and bubbled over. Janet ran to its edge.

Curled up within it, like a sleeping child, was Tam.

She had done it. He was free.

Janet hauled Tam up out of the well, took off her cloak and wrapped it around him.

'Are you hurt?' he asked. 'I'm so sorry, Janet, please tell me you're not hurt.'

He fussed over her, checking her for scratches and bites and burns, but no harm had come to her, just as he had said.

'Janet, I–'

Before Tam could say any more, the Queen of the Fairies rode into view.

Janet could only stare. The Fairy Queen wore silver, gold and polished bone. She shone like the moon.

'You have done well, Janet,' said the Queen. 'You have earned your prize. Had I known there was such strength in you, I would have plucked out Tam's eyes, so he never saw you.

'But no matter. I shall give another to Hell in his place. Think on that, Janet, when you nurse your babe in the quiet of the night. Think on that.'

The Queen and her retinue rode away. Janet took Tam's hand and led him home to Carterhaugh, his child within her. Many have wondered what became of them afterwards, but none are left who know. [1]

---

1. *This is one of the best known Scottish fairy stories. The story is derived from a ballad which exists in many variants. The scene in which Janet holds Tam as he undergoes a series of transformations is seen in many stories.*

   The story strikes a note which resonates even now; it has been retold in countless novels, comics and songs. The bestselling author Sarah J. Maas used the story as the basis of her recent series, A Court of Roses and Thorns.

4

ORANGEY & APPLEY

In a village in the North-East of Scotland, there once lived a woodcutter. He had a wife and daughter, and his daughter's name was Appley. They were a happy family until the woodcutter's wife took ill one winter. Her strength sapped away, and just as the first snowdrops emerged, she died.

Her husband and daughter grieved her terribly, but time eased their pain. A few years later, the woodcutter met a woman who won his heart. They married and she moved into his house, along with her own daughter, whose name was Orangey.

Orangey and Appley were now stepsisters. They were about the same age, and got on well enough, but there was one problem.

Appley's stepmother hated her. Seeing Appley reminded

her that the woodcutter had loved another woman before her. So, she made Appley's life a misery. Appley was forced to do all the most unpleasant jobs around the house, and at mealtimes Appley was given less food than the others.

Every day was a trial for Appley. She did her best, hoping to please her stepmother and win her favour, but it never worked, and she was deeply unhappy. Things remained this way for years, until one cold day in winter.

'Appley!' called the stepmother. 'Come here!'

Appley had been scrubbing the fireplace. She put down her brush and went through to the kitchen.

'Take this,' said her stepmother, handing her a finely painted jug, 'and fill it up from the well. And just you mind, it belonged to my mother, so be careful!'

Appley took the jug from her stepmother. She left the house and walked to the well at the edge of the woods. She filled up the jug, and was on her way home when she tripped on a root. The jug flew from her hands, landed on a stone and smashed.

Appley was terrified of what her stepmother would do. Would she get a row? Would she be sent to bed without supper? Well, putting it off wouldn't help. She gathered up the pieces of the jug and went home.

'I'm sorry,' said Appley to her stepmother. 'I tripped and broke your mother's jug.'

The stepmother looked at the pieces of the jug in horror. She put down her rolling pin.

Appley didn't get a row.

She wasn't sent to bed without supper.

The stepmother took her husband's axe from the wall, swung it at Appley and cut her head off. She chopped her up into tiny pieces, which she put into the soup that she was making for the family dinner. It would have been a vegetable soup, but now it was a meat soup.

Orangey had been playing by the river. She returned home and said to her mother, 'Where is Appley?'

'She went out for a walk,' said Orangey's mother. 'Go and play in front of the fire until dinner's ready.'

So Orangey went and played in front of the fire.

The woodcutter came home. He kissed his wife and step-daughter and said, 'Where is Appley?'

'Appley went out for a walk,' said his wife with a sweet smile. 'I'm sure she'll be back soon. Sit down, the soup is almost ready.'

'It smells delicious,' said the woodcutter.

The soup was soon ready. Orangey, the woodcutter and his wife sat down at the table to eat.

'Mmm,' said the woodcutter. 'This soup is wonderful. What kind of meat is it?'

'It's my secret recipe,' said his wife. 'You just eat up.'

They were all happily chewing and slurping when a little bone floated to the surface of the woodcutter's soup.

He dropped his spoon.

The bone had a ring on it. It was Appley's ring.

In that moment, the woodcutter realised why Appley hadn't come home from her walk. He understood where the meat for their soup had come from.

'You.. you cooked her!' he cried in horror. 'You killed Appley and put her in the soup!'

'She deserved it!' said his wife. 'She smashed my best jug!'

The woodcutter was distraught. He ran to the outhouse to make himself sick, then sat down in front of the fire and cried. His wife sat at the table, calmly finishing off her soup. She even had seconds.

Orangey cried with her father, late into the night. When she had no more tears left, she stood up, gathered up the little pieces of her sister's bones and took them outside.

Orangey took the bones to a spot which Appley had always liked, a pair of marble stones at the far end of the garden. She dug a hole and buried her sister's bones between the stones. After saying goodbye to her sister and crying some more, she went to bed.

Later that night, as the moon shone down upon the village, the earth between the two stones trembled.

From out of the earth came a milk-white dove, or a 'doo'

as we say in Scotland. It hopped about, cleaned the dirt from its wings and flew into the forest.

Winter deepened. Snow fell day after day, covering the village and the woods in a white mantle. The days grew shorter and darker, but the people of the village were happy, for Christmas was coming.

On Christmas Eve, not long after sunset, the white dove flew out of the forest and into the village.

The dove flew through the window of the toy shop and landed on the counter. It cooed, and the shopkeeper came through from the back of the shop.

'Oh my,' he said. 'What a beautiful doo you are.'

It cooed again and sang to the shopkeeper.

> My mummy killed me,
> My daddy ate me,
> My sister Orangey licked my bones,
> And buried me 'tween two marble stones,
> And I turned into a milk-white doo, doo.

'Goodness me,' said the shopkeeper. 'That's a dreadful tale to hear at Christmas. Let me give you this.'

He gave a doll to the dove. The dove took the doll's arm between its feet and flew away.

Not long after that, a watchmaker was counting up his takings when a dove flew in through his shop window and land on the counter.

'You are a beauty,' he said to the dove. The dove cooed at him and sang its song.

> My mummy killed me,
> My daddy ate me,
> My sister Orangey licked my bones,
> And buried me 'tween two marble stones,
> And I turned into a milk-white doo, doo.

'Really?' said the watchmaker. 'Is that so? Well, let me give you this.' He took a beautiful gold watch from his cabinet and gave it to the dove, which flew away with the watch clasped between its feet.

A little later, a blacksmith was just about to close the door of his forge when the dove flew in and landed on an axe-handle.

'Hello,' he said. 'What are you doing in here?'

The dove sang to him.

> My mummy killed me,
> My daddy ate me,
> My sister Orangey licked my bones,
> And buried me 'tween two marble stones,
> And I turned into a milk-white doo, doo.

'That's an awful thing to happen,' said the blacksmith. 'Let me give you a present. That axe you're perched upon; it's yours.'

The dove cooed a thank you to the blacksmith. With a great effort, it lifted the axe and flew away.

Back in the woodcutter's house, everything was set for Christmas. Stockings hung from the mantelpiece and a turkey waited in the pantry. The family sat in silence around the fire. There had been little joy in their home since Appley died.

All of a sudden, they heard a voice coming from the fireplace.

'Orangey,' sang the voice.

'Who is that?' said Orangey. 'Is that... is that you, Appley?'

'Yes, it's me. I've got a present for you. Come to the fire-place. Put out the fire and hold out your hands.'

Orangey dashed to the fireplace. Ignoring her mother's protests, she raked the fire and poured water over it until the flames died. She held her hands out over the embers.

Into her hands dropped a doll.

'Oh, thank you!' she said with a beaming smile. 'Thank you, Appley!'

'You're welcome,' said the voice. 'Daddy, I have a present for you. Come to the fireplace and hold out your hands.'

Her father did as asked. Into his hands fell a gold watch.

'This is marvellous! Thank you, Appley!' he said.

'Mummy,' said the voice. 'It's your turn now. I have a special present for you.'

Appley's stepmother was a greedy woman. Without a second thought, she got up from her chair and knelt in front of the fireplace.

'Closer,' said the voice.

The stepmother leant in closer.

'Closer. Closer. Closer...' said the voice, until the step-mother's head was over the embers of the fire.

'I can't go any further,' she said.

That was when the dove, who was up on the roof, gave the stepmother her present. She dropped the axe. It flew down the chimney and chopped the stepmother's head right off.

That was the end of the stepmother. They buried her in the garden. The following day, the woodcutter, Orangery and the doo ate Christmas dinner together. They considered cooking the stepmother, but decided to stick to turkey. [1]

---

1. *I heard this story from Jess Smith, a Traveller storyteller who grew up on a bus with her many siblings and was raised on stories. It is a variant of the singing bone story. In many such stories, the protagonist is murdered by a sibling, and their bones sing of the murder, sometimes after being made into an instrument.*

   Jess has a number of fascinating books available about her life and about Traveller culture.

5

DEATH IN A NUT

A boy called Jack once lived on the west coast of Argyll with his mother. They lived on a croft where they grew potatoes, turnips and carrots, and they kept a goat for milking and some hens for their eggs.

Every morning, Jack left the house early to go walking on the beach before breakfast. He would search for crabs among the rock pools and look for driftwood to bring home for the fire.

One morning in summer, Jack was strolling along the shore when he saw a man walking towards him. He wore a long black coat and had black hair, a black beard and a black hat. His trousers and boots were black too, and in his hand he held a scythe.

The black-clad man approached Jack. His gaze turned

Jack's blood to ice.

'What's your name?' asked the man, his voice as cold and sharp as his scythe.

'Jack,' said Jack. 'What's your name?'

'Death,' said the man.

The crash of the surf became a whisper.

'I wonder if you could help me, Jack,' said Death, stroking his scythe-blade. 'I'm looking for someone.'

'Who are you looking for?'

'Your mother.'

'My... my mother?'

Yes,' said Death. 'I know your house is near here, but I'm not sure exactly where. Be a good lad and point me in the right direction.'

Jack came to his senses. The surf was singing, gulls were screeching and he wasn't going to let Death take his mother.

Jack threw himself at Death. Death was tall and strong, but Jack was quick and took him by surprise. He tackled Death, bringing him down to the ground. Jack was the best wrestler among the boys in his village, and he put his skills to good use. He wrapped himself around Death, pinning him down so that he couldn't move a single limb.

What to do now? He couldn't let Death go. Jack looked around for a bit of rope to bind Death with, but there was none to be seen. He did, however, see a hazelnut shell.

That gave him an idea.

Jack squeezed Death and folded him over. He folded

Death, again and again, until he could fit him in the palm of his hand. When that was done, he grabbed the hazelnut shell and stuffed Death into it. He pressed the shell closed and put it into his pocket.

Death's scythe still lay on the sand. Jack hid it in a cave and strode home, whistling a merry tune.

Jack arrived home to find his mother boiling water for tea over the fire.

'Good morning, Jack,' she said. 'Did you find anything interesting at the beach?'

'No,' said Jack.

'Why are you looking at me like that, Jack?'

Jack realised he was staring at his mother. She would be dead now if hadn't put Death in the nut. It made him realise how much he loved her. He ran over to her and kissed her cheek.

'Would you like eggs for breakfast, mother? I'll make them.'

'I would, thank you,' said Jack's mother, touched by his sudden show of affection.

Jack went out to the hen-house and returned with four eggs. He removed the whistling kettle from the hook over the fire, and put the girdle in its place. After smearing butter over the girdle, he took an egg and cracked it off the side; but the egg wouldn't crack.

'They're tough eggs, these,' said Jack. He tried again, harder, but still the egg wouldn't crack. Jack went on hitting the egg against the girdle, harder and harder, but not a sliver of a crack did he make in the eggshell.

'Let me have a go,' said Jack's mother. She had no luck either. 'There must be something wrong with that egg. Try another one,' she said.

Jack tried another egg and fared no better. It was getting frustrating now. He held the egg aloft and brought it smashing down on the girdle with all his strength. No good. He took a knife from a drawer and tried that; no good. Cursing under his breath, Jack took a hammer from a drawer, set the egg down on the kitchen worktop and beat the egg with the hammer until he had no strength left.

'Maybe we'd better have carrots instead,' said Jack's mother. 'Away out and get some carrots from the garden.'

Jack did as his mother asked and returned with some big, fat carrots.

'Chop them up and fry them,' said Jack's mother. Jack washed the carrots, took the knife and began to chop them; only the knife wouldn't go through them.

'The carrots too?' said Jack's mother. 'This is very strange.'

She had a try, but neither of them could get the knife's blade through the carrots.

'We must have used up all of our strength somehow,' said Jack's mother. 'I know what to do. Take some money from the jar and go to the butcher's. He's a strong man, he'll never run out of strength; and even if he does, he's got that big meat cleaver of his. It could chop through anything. Get some sausages and we'll have them for breakfast.'

Jack took a few coins from the money jar and headed into the village. He went into the butcher's shop and asked for a string of sausages.

'Jack, I'd love to sell you a string of sausages,' said the butcher. 'But I can't.'

'Why not?' asked Jack.

'Watch.' The butcher lay a long string of sausages on the counter. He took his mighty cleaver in hand and brought it down on the string between two sausages. When he lifted the cleaver, Jack saw that the sausages remained attached.

'It's the same with the steak,' said the butcher, shaking his head. He put some steak meat on the counter, lifted his cleaver up high and brought it smashing down on the meat. It bounced off the meat.

'I'd have more luck chopping iron than meat today,' said the butcher.

'I couldn't crack an egg back at home,' said Jack. 'Or cut a carrot.'

The butcher shook his head again. 'Something strange is going on, Jack. It's as if... as if nothing will die.'

With that, Jack understood what had happened.

Jack ran out of the butcher's shop and all the way home. He burst into his house to find his mother drinking tea in front of the fire.

'Did you get the sausages, Jack?'

'Mother, I've done something I shouldn't have done.'

Jack sat down and told his mother about his meeting with Death.

'Oh, Jack,' said his mother when he'd finished. 'That was very brave, what you did. But it was wrong.

'Death is painful, Jack. But the world needs death. Death is what keeps the world alive. I wish my time hadn't come so soon, but if it's my time, it's my time. You have to let it be.'

Jack hugged his mother. They wept together for a good, long time. Eventually, Jack stood up, took a deep breath, turned and left the house.

He returned to the beach and found Death's scythe where he'd hidden it in the sea-cave. With a heavy heart, Jack reached into his pocket, took out the nut and opened it up.

Death shot out and landed on the sand. He unfolded until he was his regular size and got to his feet. The look he gave Jack could have melted bones.

'...Sorry, Death.' said Jack. 'Here's your scythe.'

Death snatched his scythe from Jack's hand.

'You've got some nerve, lad,' said Death.

'I'm sorry,' said Jack. 'I know what I did was wrong. The world needs you.'

'It does,' said Death. 'Whether it needs you is another matter.'

'I don't mind if you take me,' said Jack. 'Just don't take my mother.'

'Your mother?'

'Yes,' said Jack. 'You said you were going to see her.'

Death burst out laughing.

'Oh, Jack. You daft wee lad.' He cuffed Jack over the head. 'I was only going to stop in and see your mother for a cup of tea!'

'Really?'

'Yes! It's not her time yet. I'm on my way to see an old man in the next village. He's on his last legs; he's looking forward to seeing me.'

Jack felt rather foolish. 'Oh,' he said. 'Well, in that case, I'll walk you to the house.'

Jack took Death home to see his mother, who made them all a cup of tea and some eggs on toast. They had a good gossip before Death went on his way. [1]

---

1. *Jack stories are very popular in Scotland, particularly among the Travellers. They are also told a lot in England, and have taken root over the water in Appalachia. The most famous is* Jack and The Beanstalk. *The Jack O' Lanterns of Halloween are named after a Jack tale. In archetypal terms, Jack is usually classed as a trickster, like Loki or Coyote, but he also has a hint of*

the Divine Child in him; an archetype expressed in Baby Krishna and Jesus among others.

I don't tell many Jack stories myself, but I love this one. It was told a lot by Duncan Williamson, a legendary Traveller storyteller who was believed to have gathered over 3000 stories and 3000 songs. I heard this version from Donald Smith, the director of the Scottish International Storytelling Festival and a brilliant author and storyteller.

6

THE BATTLE OF THE BIRDS

I n an age long past, the animals and birds of Scotland would hold a tournament each year, to decide who would be their King or Queen on the next year. This tournament was known as the Battle of the Birds.

There was once a Scottish king who was desperate to see the battle, but too old to travel there himself. So, he sent his son to watch the tournament and report back to him.

The Prince left his father's castle and travelled out to the wild places. He passed the last village and made his way into the mountains. After many days, he heard a great tumult of screeching, roaring, howling and cawing. He had reached the site of the Battle of the Birds.

The tourney was held in a hollow, high among the mountains, at the edge of a great waterfall. The pool was full of salmon and otters, and the air was full of eagles, kites, crows and birds of all kinds. On the grass were wolves, bears, boars, badgers and every other Scottish creature.

None of them paid the Prince any heed; they were intent upon watching the final battle. He weaved his way through the throng and reached the front. There on the grass before him, the two finalists fought.

The duel was between a snake and an enormous raven, and it looked to be almost over. Blood dripped from the raven's wounds as it hopped away from the advancing serpent.

The snake was driving the raven towards the Prince.

As he watched, the Prince slowly and quietly unsheathed his sword. None of the animals seemed to notice; except for the raven, which cocked its eye at him, just for a moment.

The snake made its last lunge. Thinking that the raven was finished, it didn't strike with all its strength.

The raven leapt over the lunge and took to the air. The snake twisted as the Prince darted forward, swung his sword and cut off its head.

The animals and birds cried out in a hundred voices. Was this foul play? The rules of the tourney were that no animal could help another; they did not speak of men.

The raven cried victory. He flew down and said to the Prince, 'Climb upon my back, and I shall take you from here.'

The Prince climbed onto the raven's back. It beat its wings and carried him into the sky and away from the battle. Over seven bens, seven glens and seven mountain moors they flew, until, in the golden light of evening, they reached a house.

'This is my sister's house,' said the raven as they landed. 'When she asks you, say that you saw her likeness at the battle, and you shall be well rewarded.'

The Prince thanked the raven and went into the house. A dark-haired woman awaited him inside.

'Where have you come from?' she asked him.

'I have come from the Battle of the Birds,' he answered.

'Did you see my likeness there?'

'I did.'

She smiled at that, and prepared for him a fine meal. After eating together, she bathed him and invited him into her bed.

In the morning, he left the house and saw the raven outside. Again, they flew over seven bens, seven glens and seven mountain moors, and again the raven took him to a house where one of his sisters lived.

In went the Prince. A dark-haired woman sat by the fire.

'Where have you come from?' she asked him.

'I have come from the Battle of the Birds,' he answered.

'Did you see my likeness there?'

'I did.'

The raven's sister was pleased. She gave him the best of every food, the best of every drink, a hot bath and a warm bed to share.

The following morning, he went outside expecting to see

the raven awaiting him. Instead, he saw a fair-faced, sharp-eyed young man, who held a bundle in his arms.

'Where is the raven?' asked the Prince.

'You will not see him again. I was the raven, for I was put under a spell many moons ago. I would only be free when I became a king, and thanks to you, that time has come. In thanks, I give you this.'

He put the bundle into the Prince's hands.

'Go back to your people,' said the young man, 'and only open the bundle in the place you most wish to dwell.'

The Prince thanked the young man and set off towards home. On foot he crossed the bens, glens and moors that he had flown over, and again he stopped each night with his friend's sisters.

At length, he spied the turrets of his father's castle in the distance.

'I know where I will open this bundle,' he said. 'In the green hollow by my father's castle, where I used to play as a boy.'

He carried on until he came to a wood. The air there was heavy and made him yawn. As he walked, the bundle grew heavy in his hands.

'I have carried my bundle all this way,' he said to himself, 'and I still don't know what's inside it. Well, I mustn't open it, but surely it wouldn't hurt to take a peek inside.'

Before he could think better of it, the Prince opened the bundle just enough to peek inside.

The moment he did so, the bundle flew from his arms and burst open. Out of it came an entire castle. The castle crashed down on the ground, flattening the trees and shaking the ground so that the Prince fell upon his face.

He leapt up and gazed at the battlements and turrets, the grand spires and fluttering flags of his castle. It was the most wondrous sight he had ever beheld. He only wished he had opened the bundle in the hollow by his father's castle.

As he stood there, the ground shook again. Through the forest came a black-bearded, balding giant, who was as tall as the walls of his castle.

'Well, well,' said the giant. 'That's quite a castle, and it wasn't here yesterday.'

'I was given a bundle with the castle in it,' said the Prince. 'I opened it here by accident.'

'Did you now? Well, there's not much you can do about that, but there's plenty I can do about it. I can put this castle back in the bundle for you.'

'And what would you ask in return?' said the Prince.

'I would ask that when your firstborn son reaches seven years of age, you give him to me.'

The Prince laughed. He would never give his firstborn son, his heir, to this giant. And yet... imagine if his castle was right by his father's castle, in the centre of the kingdom, where all would see and admire it. What good was a castle if it was hidden in a deep, dank wood? It might do his son good to grow up in the giant's house. Surely the giant wouldn't harm him?

'Very well,' said the Prince.

In a flash, the giant was pulling down walls, flattening turrets and squeezing the castle back into the bundle. He pressed the bundle into the Prince's hands.

'Your firstborn son,' said the giant. 'Don't forget.'

The Prince left the wood and opened the bundle in the place he had intended. The castle appeared just as before, and this time he entered it. Soldiers and servants stood in line to greet him, and beyond them all stood a beautiful maiden wearing a wedding dress.

'Marry me this night,' she said to him, 'and all shall be well with you.'

He saw no reason to refuse her. They married that night and lived in the castle together. When the Prince's father died, they became King and Queen of the realm, and their castle was the centre of the kingdom.

The Queen became pregnant, and the next summer she gave birth to their first child.

It was a boy.

While the people cheered and drank toasts in the inns, the King fretted, for he knew that the giant would come for his son. What if the giant did plan to harm him? He told his wife. She was furious with him, and as frightened as he was.

All too quickly, the Prince's seventh birthday came. On that morning, as the Prince played with his wooden sword while his father and mother sat staring into their wine cups, they felt the ground shake beneath their feet.

The King and Queen looked at one another.

'It must be done,' said the Queen.

The King nodded. He rose from his chair.

Down to the kitchens he went, where the cook was bent over a roaring oven. The cook's son sat on the floor at his side, kneading bread.

'Cook,' said the King, 'I have need of your son.'

'Is he in trouble, sire?' said the cook. 'I'll deal with him if he is, you mark my words.'

'No,' said the King, not meeting the cook's eye. 'He's not in trouble. Come along now, boy.'

The cook's son put his doughy hand in the King's hand. The King led him to his own son's chambers, where he washed the boy's hands and face, and dressed him in the young Prince's clothes. That done, he led the boy out of the castle and onto the road, where the giant stood waiting.

'This is your son?' said the giant.

'It is,' said the King.

'Then give him to me.'

The giant picked up the boy and put him on his shoulder. He turned and walked away into the forest.

The cook's son thought it was a fine thing to see the world from a giant's shoulder. As he bounced along, giggling and whooping, the giant said to him, 'Boy, let me give you something.'

He took from his belt a golden sceptre and put it in the boy's hand.

'Tell me, boy. What would your father do with this?' asked the giant.

'He would whack the dogs and cats with it,' said the boy, swishing the sceptre, 'to get them away from the King's meat.'

'You are not the King's son,' said the giant.

'I am the cook's son,' said the boy.

The giant's face turned red. He lifted the boy from his shoulder and dashed his brains out against a tree.

The giant returned to the castle, roaring his rage. He smashed his fist against the gates and brought them crashing down.

'Bring me the boy you promised me!' he bellowed, his voice shaking the stones. 'Bring me the boy you promised me!'

Within their chambers, the King and Queen held and comforted their son.

'Am I the boy who was promised to the giant?' he asked his parents.

'No,' said his father, 'he is talking about the butler's son.'

The King rang for the butler and told him to dress his own son in the Prince's clothes. When that was done, the King led the butler's son out to meet the giant on the road.

'This is your son?' asked the giant.

'It is,' said the King.

The giant snatched the butler's son and took him away. The butler's son trembled as he sat upon the giant's shoulder, fearing he would fall.

'Tell me,' said the giant as he lumbered through the forest, 'what would your father do with this?' He put the gold sceptre into the boy's hand.

'Why, my father would beat the cats and dogs with it, to stop them from knocking over the King's cups.'

'You are not the King's son!'

The giant seized the boy, swung him against a tree and smashed his skull. Leaving the boy's body there, he turned and ran back the way he came.

Within the castle, the King, Queen and Prince felt the ground shake beneath them.

Chunks of stone came crashing down around them. The giant was pounding at the castle, tearing it apart with his fists. He tore off turrets and swung them like clubs until the castle was in ruins.

'Bring me the boy!' the giant howled. 'Bring me the boy!'

The King came running through the ruins.

'Stop! Stop! Here he is!' he shouted, climbing over the rubble with his son slung over his shoulder.

'This is really him?' said the giant.

'I swear it,' said the King.

The giant seemed satisfied. He took the screaming child from the King and carried him away.

The giant had his own castle, which stood on an island amid a mighty river surrounded by towering mountains.

The Prince grew up in the giant's castle. He wandered the castle's vast corridors and dusty chambers. He stood on the bridge to watch enormous fish leap from the water as they hunted eagles. The giant told the Prince that when he came of age, he would marry one of the giant's two beautiful daughters. The Prince saw them occasionally, but they never spoke to him, and it was a lonely life he led.

From time to time, the Prince would hear singing coming from somewhere in the castle at night. A great smile would light up his face, for the strange, beautiful singing was the only thing that made him happy. He would leave his chamber and go wandering through the castle, searching for the source of the sound, but he never found it.

Days, weeks and years groaned by. The Prince was no longer a boy but a young man when he awoke one evening to hear the singing he loved. He leapt out of bed. It seemed to be louder and closer than ever before.

The Prince searched every corridor and chamber. He went outside to stand beneath the stars and listen. Looking back at the castle, he saw a light in a high turret.

Back into the castle he went. He searched the high, dusty chambers. Though he had searched them many times, he saw a door that he hadn't noticed before.

The Prince turned the door handle. He opened the door and came face to face with the singer.

It was one of the giant's daughters.

'I am the giant's third daughter,' she said. 'He keeps me hidden up here because he doesn't want you to marry me. But I want to marry you.'

The Prince had fallen in love with the girl back when he first heard her singing.

'I want to marry you,' he said.

'Then listen carefully,' said the girl. 'Tomorrow, my father will present my sisters to you, and ask which of them you wish to marry. Say that you wish to marry me, his youngest daughter. You must then do as he asks of you.'

The Prince agreed. He returned to his chamber, and in the morning the giant called for him.

The giant stood in the hall with his two eldest daughters at his side. The girls glared at the Prince.

'The time has come for you to marry,' said the giant. 'Which of my daughters do you wish to take as your bride?'

'I wish to marry your youngest daughter,' said the Prince.

The giant threw back his head and roared, making the entire castle shake.

'Very well,' said the giant. 'If you complete the three tasks I set for you, you may marry my youngest daughter. And if you don't...' He bent down, bringing his face close to the Prince. 'If you don't, I shall you beat you until you are nothing but blood and bone-dust.'

The giant led the Prince out to the byre, where he kept his herd of a hundred cattle.

Inside the byre, the Prince held his nose as he gazed around him. He had never been in there; the smell had always put him off. Now he understood why it smelt so bad. The byre was the filthiest place he had ever seen, full of heaps of dung taller than he was.

'It's seven years since I last cleaned the byre,' said the giant. 'If you wish to marry my youngest daughter, you must clean it today. I shall return at nightfall, and if I cannot roll an apple across the floor, so that it reaches the far end of the byre unblemished, you will not see the morning.' With that, the giant left.

There was nothing for it but to get started. The Prince found a spade and set to work, but it was hopeless. Come noon, he paused for breath. He still couldn't even see the floor in the spot where he'd been working.

The giant's youngest daughter appeared at his side.

'Why don't you rest for a while?' she said. 'I can take over.'

The Prince gratefully accepted. He went outside and lay down on the grass. When he woke up, he leapt to his feet. The sun was red and sinking in the sky; he had been asleep all afternoon!

He returned to the byre and saw that all his work had been done. The dung was gone and the floor gleamed like silver. The giant's youngest daughter was nowhere to be seen.

The ground shook; the giant appeared at his side.

'I cleaned the byre,' said the Prince.

'Somebody cleaned the byre,' said the giant. 'But I don't think it was you.'

'It wasn't you,' said the Prince.

'Hmph!' the giant snorted and took an apple from his pocket. He knelt down and rolled it across the floor. He crossed the byre, picked it up and saw that it was unblemished.

'Come here tomorrow, boy,' said the giant. 'And we will see if your luck holds.'

The Prince met the giant outside the byre the next morning.

'Now that my byre is clean and sparkling, I think it deserves a new thatch to match the floor,' said the giant.

'Today, I want you to thatch my byre with bird-down; and every feather must be of a different colour. Succeed, and you shall marry your heart's desire. Fail, and your bone-dust will scatter in the wind.'

Shaking his head, the Prince went to his chamber to retrieve his sling. He set off over the bridge and into the glens, where by noon he had only shot down a pigeon, a magpie and a corncrake. It was hopeless.

He heard a yell, and saw the giant's youngest daughter heading towards him.

'Well done,' she said as she inspected his catch. 'Why don't you take a break now? I'll take over.'

The Prince was wise enough not to argue. He lay down to sleep on the hillside, and when he woke up, he saw an enormous heap of feathers, each one of a different hue.

'Let's fetch a sack and get these to the byre,' said the giant's youngest daughter.

The giant came home that evening. He saw that the byre had been thatched with feathers of a thousand hues.

'I thatched the byre,' said the Prince, who stood admiring it.

'Somebody thatched the byre,' said the giant.

'You didn't thatch the byre,' said the Prince.

The giant snarled at the Prince but didn't argue. 'Well, be sure to get a good sleep tonight, Prince,' said the giant. 'I shall have another task for you tomorrow.'

Tomorrow came. The giant led the Prince across the

bridge to a woodland. He stopped beneath a pine tree, the tallest tree to be seen. The Prince could barely see its top; trying to do so gave him a stiff neck.

'There is a magpie's nest at the top of the tree,' said the giant, 'with five eggs in it. If you wish to marry my youngest daughter, you must bring me those five eggs with not a crack in them. You know the price of failure.' The giant laughed and stomped away.

The Prince studied the tree. There was not a single branch to grab hold of. He wrapped his arms around the tree and tried to shimmy up it using his knees, but he slid down as if the tree was a greased pole. Over and over he tried this, but to no avail.

'It's no good,' he said as noon came. 'The giant is going to crack my skull.'

Just as he said this, the giant's youngest daughter appeared at his side.

'You can climb the tree,' she said. 'You just need a little help.'

She jabbed her fingers into the bark of the tree with such force that she left two holes in its bark. Laughing, she made another two above them. She put her hands and feet into the first holes she had made, and climbed up to make more holes. The giant's youngest daughter climbed all the way up the tree in this fashion, and when she reached the top she climbed back down.

'I have made a ladder for you,' she said. 'But it has cost

me.' She held up her hands and he saw that one of her fingers had broken off. 'Don't make a fuss,' she said. 'Go and get the magpie's eggs.'

The Prince thanked her and put his feet and hands in the lowermost holes. He climbed up and soon was dizzyingly high. The tree was taller than the castle, and the wind buffeted it as he neared the top.

'Don't look down!' shouted the giant's daughter. 'Just keep going!'

His muscles aching, the terrified Prince reached the top. There was the nest, the five spotted eggs within it. He wrapped them in a cloth, slipped them carefully into his pocket and climbed back down.

The giant's daughter was waiting for him.

'Your wedding day is tomorrow,' she said. 'My father has invited guests from every corner of the world. There shall be feasting and dancing, and in the evening, he shall offer you my sisters and I to choose from. We will marry, if you know which sister is me.'

They returned to the castle. The giant's daughter returned to her chamber and the Prince showed the eggs to the giant, who didn't look pleased.

'Very well,' said the giant. 'You shall marry tomorrow, although which of my daughters you will marry is still to be seen.'

The Prince awoke to the beating of drums and the blaring of horns. He looked out of his chamber window to see a procession of men, birds and beasts crossing the bridge and entering the castle.

He washed his face, put on his finest clothes and went downstairs to join the revelry. Fairy-folk feasted at tables heaped with food. Horse-headed men danced with bearded women to music played by a band of cats. The Prince feasted in the feasting hall, danced in the dancing hall and wandered among the guests, searching for the giant's youngest daughter; but he never saw her or her sisters.

Evening shadows crept into the feasting hall. The giant strode in, clapped his hands and all fell silent.

'It is time for my foster-son to choose his bride,' he said. The drunken guests cheered and banged their cups on the tables.

A door opened, and through it came the giant's three daughters. They were dressed identically in silver-white gowns. Their hair was arranged identically; they wore the same jewellery and the same expression on their faces.

The Prince stood and approached them. He cared nothing for the giant's eldest daughters, and he loved the giant's youngest daughter. For all that, he could not tell her apart from her sisters.

Except that she was missing a finger.

'I shall marry this one,' said the Prince, standing before the daughter with the missing finger.

She smiled at him. He turned to look at the giant.

'Very well,' said the giant. 'Take her to your chamber.'

Some guests cheered and others stayed silent as the Prince and his bride left the feasting hall. They made their way to the Prince's bedchamber and closed the door behind them. Through the window, the Prince could see the guests leaving.

'I love you–' he began, but his bride interrupted him.

'He will murder us,' she said.

'What?'

'My father will wait until we are asleep, before coming in here and murdering us,' she said.

'What should we do?'

The youngest daughter took an apple and a knife from a hidden pocket in her dress. She cut the apple into nine slices, and put two at the head of the bed and two at the foot of the bed.

'Follow me,' she said, 'and don't let anyone see you.'

They left the chamber and slipped through the castle, staying among the shadows. The youngest daughter laid down two slices of apple by the kitchen doors and two more at the gates. She led the Prince to the stables.

They saddled a blue-grey filly, climbed into the saddle and led her out into the darkness. As they crossed the bridge, the giant's daughter dropped the final slice of apple.

Not long afterwards, the giant crept through the corridors to the Prince's bedchamber, his axe in his hand.

He bent down and softly rapped his knuckle against the door. 'Are you awake?' he asked, his voice as soft as silk.

'Yes, we are awake,' said the slices of apple at the top of the bed.

The giant shook his head and went back to his chambers.

A little while later, he returned.

'Are you awake?' he asked.

'Yes, we are awake,' said the slices of apple at the foot of the bed.

The giant left.

When he returned, he asked again, 'Are you awake?' When no-one answered, he smashed the door down with his foot. The bedchamber was empty.

'They must have gone to the kitchen to have something to eat,' he told himself. He went to the kitchen and knocked on the kitchen door. 'My children, are you in there?' he asked.

'Yes, we are in here eating,' said the slices of apple on the other side of the door.

The giant swore and returned to his chambers. Soon he returned, and when no-one answered his question, he opened the kitchen door to find no-one within.

Now, he was beginning to worry. He returned to the Prince's chamber; they weren't there. He went to the main door, knocked on it and said, 'My children, are you out there?'

'Yes,' said the slices of apple, 'we've come out to see the stars.'

The giant couldn't wait any longer. He opened the door and when he saw no-one there, he knew he'd been tricked. He roared and beat the ground with his fists, and his roars were heard in every corner of the world.

Down dark roads the filly raced. Night turned to half-light, which turned to light.

'My father's breath is burning my back,' said the giant's daughter. 'Put your hand in the filly's left ear.'

The Prince did so. He pulled out the twig of a sloe tree, just as he felt the ground shake and heard the giant's footsteps behind them.

'Throw it down behind us!' shouted the giant's daughter.

He threw it down as the giant entered the glen they were leaving. A forest shot up all through the glen. Its trees were packed tightly together, and the ground was covered in such dense bramble bushes that even a weasel couldn't have slipped through.

The giant stopped and examined the forest. He would have to cut his way through with an axe; but he had left his axe at home, so that he could run faster. He ran all the way back to his castle, collected his axe, returned to the wood and hacked a path through it.

By the time he had finished, he was panting and covered in sweat.

'I'll leave my axe here, so I can run faster,' he said to himself.

'If you do that, I will steal it,' said a hoodie crow that was watching him from the treetops.

The giant swore at the crow and tried to catch it and crush it, but he couldn't. He went all the way home with his axe before returning to the chase.

Morning turned to noon as the sun climbed the sky. The Prince and his bride tore across the land on the tireless filly's back.

'I can feel my father's breath on my back again,' said the giant's daughter as the moor beneath them shook. 'Put your hand in her right ear!'

The Prince found in the filly's ear a little grey rock.

'Throw it down behind us!' said the giant's daughter.

The Prince twisted round. He saw the giant sprinting towards them over the moor and threw down the rock. A towering mass of jagged rocks shot up, reaching all the way to the clouds.

The giant stopped before them. He put his hand to the nearest rock and it cut his fingers. 'This mountain is too sharp to climb,' he said. 'I shall need to go home and get my lever and mattock, so I can tunnel my way through.'

He did so, and with great effort he made his tunnel.

When he was done, he said 'I shall leave my lever and mattock here.'

The hoodie crow was there too.

'I shall steal your lever and mattock if you do that,' it said. The giant ran all the way home again before resuming the chase.

Evening had come. The Prince spied his father's castle up ahead. As they galloped down the road, the giant's daughter shouted, 'My father's breath is burning my back! Reach into the filly's left ear again!'

The ground shook. Roaring rattled their bones. The Prince reached into the filly's left ear and pulled out a bladder of water. As the giant's shadow fell on them, the Prince threw the bladder down behind them. A loch appeared in its place.

The giant fell in and sank to the bottom. He swam to the surface and swam after them; but he had run far that day, and tired himself with his labours. His arms ceased to work, and his legs ceased to serve him. He sank to the bottom of the loch and drowned.

The Prince cheered. The giant's daughter gave a sad smile. She was glad he was dead, but the giant was her father, so it was a bitter joy. They dismounted the filly, and rested against a tree by the water's edge.

'I know he was family to you,' said the Prince. 'But you'll soon meet my family, and they will be your family.'

'I can't meet them yet,' said his bride. 'If I am to stay here with you, you must do one more thing for me.

'You must go alone to the castle while I wait here. Tell your family of your years at my father's castle, of our marriage and our journey here. Do not let anyone kiss you until you have finished your tale. If you do, we shall never be together again.'

The Prince could make no sense of this, but he trusted his bride. He kissed her goodbye and rode for the castle.

As the Prince rode down the road leading to the castle, people recognised him and word went ahead of him. The streets were soon lined with cheering folk. At the gates, he met his mother, father and younger siblings.

They wept with joy and crowded round him to hug and kiss him. He held them back. 'I am overjoyed to see you all,' he said, 'but if I am ever to ask you anything, I ask you this: do not kiss me.'

They retired to the feasting hall. After they had eaten, the family gathered round the fire to listen to the Prince's tale.

'The giant took me to his castle, which lay in the middle of a wide river,' began the Prince. His family listened intently, wonder and fear written on their faces, along with guilt for giving him to the giant.

He came to the part of his tale where he heard the sweet music at night. His listeners leaned in closer.

As they did so, an old hound that had been the Prince's pet came wandering in. Recognising him, she bounded up to him and licked his face.

The moment her tongue touched him, the Prince forgot he had ever met the giant's daughter.

'Yes?' said his mother. 'You heard the music, and then what?'

'Then... well, I'm not sure... I suppose nothing much happened after that.'

It was a poor ending to the story, but they couldn't get any more out of him. Everyone agreed it was time for bed. The Prince went to bed, sleep took him and when he awoke, he remembered nothing of the giant's daughter.

While the Prince settled into his father's castle, the giant's daughter waited for him.

She wandered in the forest, ate what food she could find and slept in a tree above a well. It seemed that the Prince had ignored her warning; yet she didn't give up on him.

In a village nearby, there lived a shoemaker, whose family sometimes took their water from the well above which she slept. One day, the shoemaker asked his wife to fill up their bucket from the well. She walked down the path that led through the woods to the well, and as she pulled up the bucket, she saw the face of a beautiful woman mirrored in the water.

'Why, I never knew I was so fair!' she said. 'I am too fair by far to be a shoemaker's wife, that is certain!'

Leaving the bucket, she stomped home and began smashing and breaking things, telling the shoemaker that he had cruelly tricked her by marrying her, when she should be married to a great lord.

'I'm leaving you, and the next time you see me, you shall beg to lick my shoes!' she said before storming out.

The shoemaker was perplexed. 'Daughter,' he said, 'would you go to the well, since your mother isn't feeling well?'

His daughter went through the woods to the well. She looked into the water, and as she did so, she saw the face of a beautiful woman reflected there.

'Fetch water! I should not be fetching water,' she said to herself. 'I should be a princess, with servants to see to my every need.' She returned home and repeated this to her father before packing a bag and leaving.

'Something strange is going on here,' he said.

The shoemaker put down his work and walked to the well. He saw the face of a beautiful woman mirrored in the water. Since he knew for certain that he wasn't a beautiful woman, he looked up into the trees. He saw there the giant's daughter, looking down at him from among the branches.

'What are you doing up there?' he asked her.

She told him her story. When she was done, he said, 'Well, you can't go on living in a tree. Come and work for me.'

The giant's daughter got down from the tree and went home with the shoemaker.

The shoemaker lived in a thatched cottage at the edge of his village. He made a meal for the giant's daughter and said, 'I'm in need of an apprentice.'

'I'll be your apprentice,' said the giant's daughter.

They set to work that day. She learnt to cut the leather and to hammer and stitch it into shape. At first, she only worked on the simplest of shoes. Yet she took so quickly to the work, barely looking up as the hours went by, that the shoemaker gave her more complex designs to work on. Soon, she was almost as good as he was. They started working together to create new designs, and people came from far and wide to buy their shoes.

The giant's daughter enjoyed her work and the company of the shoemaker, yet she thought always of the Prince. She didn't often leave the house where they worked, except to walk in the wood, or to visit the lake where her father had drowned. Many people came to the house, though, and they brought news with them.

One day, a group of well-dressed young men came to the shoemaker's house.

'Listen here,' said one of the men to the shoemaker. 'We are all in need of shoes, and they must be the finest shoes you've ever made. They're for a very important occasion.'

'What occasion is that?' asked the shoemaker.

'Why, the Prince's wedding, of course.'

The giant's daughter dropped her work. Her head whipped round and she stared at the young man who had spoken.

'The Prince is marrying?' she said.

The young man didn't answer; he simply stared at the shoemaker's apprentice. She was the most beautiful woman he had ever seen. His friends stared at her too; they seemed to be thinking the same thing.

'He is indeed,' said the young man eventually, 'and perhaps I am too.'

He turned to the shoemaker. 'I wish to marry your apprentice. Whatever the bride-price is, I'll pay it.'

'Be off with you!' said the shoemaker, who didn't like the man's tone. 'You can get your shoes somewhere else.'

The men argued and shouted at the shoemaker, but he wouldn't be dissuaded, so they left. After they were gone, the giant's daughter said to the shoemaker, 'I would marry him, if I could keep the bride-price for myself.'

'If you did, I wouldn't take it from you,' said the shoemaker.

She went after the men, and told the young man that she would marry him.

'Tell me where you live,' she said, 'and I'll come to your house tonight. Be sure to have my bride-price ready.'

The young man couldn't believe his luck. He gave her directions and swore he would have the money ready.

That afternoon, she set off down the road. She walked until she came to the man's house. Servants let her in and showed her to his dining hall, where they sat and ate together. Afterwards, they went to the man's bedroom.

She stood by the man's bed as he closed the door behind them.

'Is that the money?' she said, pointing to a bag on a chest by the window.

'It is,' he said.

'Then come to me.'

He grinned and stepped towards her, but couldn't move.

'I am stuck to the floor!' he said.

'Yes,' she said, 'and there you shall stay.' Kissing him on the cheek, she took the bag of coins, climbed out of the window and walked home by the light of the moon.

The next day, she set to work on a new pair of shoes. These ones were for herself.

As she worked, the second of the smartly-dressed young men came into the house.

'If your apprentice is not yet married to my friend, I would like to marry her,' he said to the shoemaker.

'I will marry you tonight, if the bride-price is high,' said the giant's daughter, not looking up from her work.

He agreed, and that night she went to his house. She ate with him, and accompanied him to his bedroom. A bag of coins lay on the bed.

'Come to me,' she said as he closed the door. Yet when he tried to go to her, he could not lift his hand from the latch.

'I am stuck to the latch!' he said.

'And so shall you remain,' said the giant's daughter. She kissed his cheek, took his money and climbed out of the window.

The next day, the third young man came to the house.

'I would like to marry your apprentice, if she is not married yet,' he said to the shoemaker.

'I will marry you tonight, if the bride-price is high,' she said, not looking up.

He agreed. She went to his house, ate with him and accompanied him to his bedroom.

'Come to me, my dearest,' she said, sitting down on the bed.

The young man grinned and sat down on the bed beside her. He leaned in to kiss her. She stood, took the money from his bedside table and went to the window. He tried to stand but could not.

'I am stuck to the bed!' he said.

'And I shall never join you in it,' she said with a sweet smile.

The giant's daughter finished her shoes the next day.

'Those are the finest shoes I've ever seen,' said the shoe-maker. They were inlaid with jewels, seamlessly stitched and as splendid as a kingfisher's wing.

'I'm leaving now,' she said. 'Thank you for everything you've taught me.' She gave him the money she'd taken from the young men, and left wearing the shoes she'd made.

The giant's daughter walked all the way to the castle. The roads were crowded with people on their way to join the wedding party, or to stare in wonder and envy at the guests.

Outside the gates, she stood among the common folk. Lords and ladies passed through the gates on horseback and in carriages.

As a group of ladies passed by in their carriage, one of them chanced to look down and see the giant's daughter.

'Stop!' she said to the driver. 'Look at that girl's shoes! She belongs with us.'

The carriage door opened and the lady called over the giant's daughter, who climbed into the carriage. Through the castle gates they went, and soon they were in the feasting hall.

Sitting at the high seat was the Prince.

The giant's daughter stared at the Prince and his bride, who wore a King's ransom of jewels around her neck.

The Prince saw her staring. He looked at her for a moment before turning back to his bride.

'Don't be downhearted,' said one of the ladies, following her gaze. 'We all wish we could marry the Prince. He was raised by a giant, you know. Would you like some mead?'

'Yes, I would,' said the giant's daughter.

The lady poured her some mead, and leapt back with a shriek as flames erupted from the cup.

The hall fell silent as everyone turned to look.

A gold pigeon and a silver pigeon flew from the cup.

The Prince, his bride and all their guests watched with open mouths as the pigeons flew around the hall. Barley fell from their wings to the floor.

The silver pigeon dropped to the ground and began to eat the barley.

'Remember to share with me,' said the gold, 'for I thatched the byre.'

'I cleaned the byre,' said the silver pigeon.

'I harried the nest,' said the gold.

'And I lost a finger,' said the silver.

The Prince stood up.

He crossed the hall and stood before the giant's daughter.

They looked into one another's eyes and smiled. Their smiles were like the sunrise after a thousand-year night.

'You cleaned the byre,' he said.

'I did.'

'You thatched the byre.'

'I did.'

'You harried the nest.'

'I did.'

'You lost a finger.'

She held up her hand to show her missing finger. 'I did,' she said.

'I remember,' said the Prince.

He pulled her towards him and kissed her.

The guests were shocked. The Prince addressed the hall, telling the guests the story he'd forgotten. Though his intended bride wasn't pleased, everyone agreed that the Prince must marry the giant's daughter.

They married there and then. The wedding went on for a whole year, and though she danced every day, the bride's shoes were so well-made that her feet never hurt for a moment. [1]

---

1. *This story comes from J.F Campbell's* Popular Tales of the West Highlands. *It was told to Campbell by a fisherman living in Argyll. Being so long, it is rarely told nowadays; I have only heard it told once, by Tom Hirons, who has a wonderful travelling off-grid storytelling theatre called Hedgespoken.*

   There are lots of elements of this tale that can be found elsewhere, such as the cleaning out of the stables, reminiscent of Hercules' labours. The bargain with the giant is more familiar to us in the tradition of Faustian bargains with the devil.

Something I love about traditional stories is the questions they leave unanswered. The battle at the beginning of the story is a great example of this. I would love to know more about this battle, and about the man who became a raven. Could our ancestors have told us more?

7

FOX & DOG

The fox was cold.

The fox was tired.

Deeply cold, and deeply tired.

It was the middle of winter. Since sunrise that morning, he'd been chased by red-coated hunters riding huge, thundering horses. It had taken all his speed and guile to evade them and their barking, slavering hounds.

Now, night had come. Horns had blown, calling the hunters home. They would go home, stable their horses and sit down to heaped dinner plates while he shivered on the cold, snowy hillside.

The fox took stock of his situation. His den was miles away. He was wet through, cold to the marrow of his bones, so cold that he couldn't imagine ever being warm again. He needed to eat, and he needed to eat soon, or else he would lie down in the snow, fall asleep and never wake up again.

He mustn't let that happen. He had to keep moving, find something to eat. The problem was, he didn't have the strength to hunt. He had no chance of catching something in his state. If he tried and failed, he would be even weaker, and would stand even less chance the next time he tried.

There was only one thing for it. He needed to go scavenging.

The fox forced himself up. He trotted through the forest until he came to a road. Out onto the road he stepped, sniffing the air before setting off downhill. He sniffed and sniffed as he went, sifting through the menagerie of smells upon the air, until he smelt what he was looking for.

The fox smelt food. Warm, delicious, human food. Peering into the dusky gloom, his sharp eyes made out the shape of a farmhouse. The smell was coming from the bins out the back. His mouth began to water as he turned onto the lane leading to the farmhouse.

Closer he came, past the barns and sheds, the smell growing stronger and stronger. He approached the house, the aromas making his head spin.

Around the house he went. There, the bins! He slipped through the shadows and...

'Oi!'

He froze. Slowly, he turned his head.

By the house, close to the back door, was another house. A tiny wooden house. The front of it stood open and sitting inside it was... well, it was a dog, but not the kind of dog that hunted him. It had shaggy brown fur, floppy ears and round, gentle eyes.

'Oi!' it said again. 'What are you?'

The fox stared at the dog. 'What... what am I?' he said.

'Aye,' said the dog. 'I've never seen a... whatever you are, before. What are you?'

'I'm a fox,' said the fox.

'Fox, eh?' said the dog. 'Nice to meet you. Tell me about yourself, then. What do you do all day? What's it like being a fox?'

'What's it like? What's it like being a fox?' the fox shook his head. 'I'll tell you what it's like, pal. Being a fox is terrible.

'You live in a den, a wee hole in the side of a hill. You're never really warm, and you have to hunt for your food. Most of the time, you're not successful, and then you're tired, and the next hunt is even harder. So you're almost always hungry. When it rains, you get wet, and when it snows, you get snowed on.

'But that's not the worst part,' he went on. 'On some dreadful days, horns ring out across the countryside. Humans get up on their horses and hunt you, with packs of hounds running before them. They hunt you all day, and if they catch you, the hounds rip you to pieces while the men and women watch; and they do all this for fun. Being a fox isn't something I would wish on anybody; except those hunters, maybe.'

The dog nodded slowly. 'Dearie me,' he said. 'That does sound dreadful. You should try being a dog.'

The fox laughed. 'Alright, then,' he said. 'Go on, tell me what it's like being a dog.'

'Ah,' said the dog with a smile and a wag of his tail. 'Being a dog, let me tell you, is absolutely wonderful.

'I've got my kennel here, that I live in. It keeps me warm and keeps the rain off, and I've got a comfy rug to sit on. The master's wife comes out in the morning and brings me a bowl of food, crunchy bits and meaty bits, it's delicious. I get another bowl of the same stuff in the evening, and in the afternoon, the master or his wife takes me out for a walk. We go down the paths and I have a good sniff about, see what's going on. They throw the ball and I catch it. It's great fun.

'Oh, and I didn't tell you about the best bit yet. The best bit is that on some cold evenings, when they're in a good mood, the master and his wife let me into the house, and I stretch out on the rug, in front of a roaring fire.' He shivered with joy at the memory. 'Oh, aye. Being a dog is the best.'

The fox had been listening carefully to all of this. The dog painted a beautiful picture, and he found himself thinking that a dog's life sounded like just what he needed. But then he noticed something.

'What's that?' asked the fox.

'What's what?'

'That thing around your neck.'

'Oh,' said the dog, 'this? This is my collar.'

'What's it for?' asked the fox.

'The chain fastens onto it.'

The fox stepped closer to the dog. He saw that the collar was attached to a chain, and that the chain was attached to the kennel.

The fox took a step back. He said to the dog, 'Do you always have that collar around your neck?'

'Aye,' said the dog.

'And is it always attached to the chain?'

'Aye,' said the dog.

The fox nodded slowly. 'I see,' he said. 'I see what's going on here.' He looked up at the house and back at the dog. 'Look, pal,' he said. 'It seems like you've got a good life here. A good life. I'm glad you're happy with it. But it's freedom and hunger for me, mate. It's freedom and hunger for me.'

The fox trotted over to the bins. He ate some leftover pie and potatoes before saying goodbye and stalking off into the night.[1]

---

1. *This is another tale told by Duncan Williamson. I love it for it simplicity, elegance and profundity. It can be found in Duncan's collection,* Flight of The Golden Bird, *but I heard it on a tape recording in the School of Scottish Studies in Edinburgh. On the recording, Duncan was sitting in a tent, puffing on a cigarette as he reeled off stories to a student of folklore.*

It was an incredible conversation to eavesdrop on. Doing so might be easier in the future; Amy Douglas, an old student of Duncan's, is currently digitising many of these recordings.

8

THE SILKIE WIFE

This story is told all over Scotland, and it is one of our most famous. In Orkney they say it happened in Orkney, and folk from Eigg say it happened on Eigg. I'm from East Lothian, so I say it happened there.

North Berwick is a pretty seaside town, close to Edinburgh and popular with tourists. In bygone days it was a quiet fishing village, and in a house by the harbour, there lived a man named Tam. Tam was a fisherman. He lived with his mother, and though he was of a marrying age, he wasn't married yet.

Back then, everyone in Scotland celebrated the summer solstice. Tam had been invited to a ceilidh at Tyninghame, a few miles down the coast. He spent the day at sea on his fishing boat, and in the evening he put on his best clothes and left the house, heading along the beaches and clifftop paths towards Tyninghame.

Tam reached the ceilidh house. He opened the door and a wall of noise nearly knocked him off his feet; the party was in full swing. He downed a mug of ale, joined in the dancing and the hours flew by.

Eventually, Tam told himself it was time to go. There was fishing to be done the following day, and he had already stayed out too late. He said his goodbyes and left the house, heading home the way he came.

It was a beautiful night to be abroad. The midsummer sky was a deep, dusky blue and lit by a thousand stars. He reached Ravensheugh Sands, a great sweeping arc of golden sand, and took off his boots to walk barefoot. A faint breeze caressed the dune-grass. Languid waves lapped the shore.

Tam walked in silence along the golden sands, listening to the music of the waves. He reached the end of the beach, where a talon of rocks reaches out into the sea, and paused when a sound reached his ears. It wasn't a sound he expected to hear on the beach in the middle of the night.

It was the sound of singing.

Tam reached the rocks. He climbed up, looked out to sea and saw the one who was singing.

On a stretch of sand ringed by black rocks, out where the outcrop met the sea, a woman was singing and dancing. She wore not a stitch of clothing. Her skin was pale, her hair was a dark brown, and her dance was like nothing Tam had ever seen.

She spun, leapt and threw herself across the sand. She laughed and sang, wailed and cried. The sun and moon, the sea and sky, all the beauty and pain of life were in her dance. She seems to feel so much sadness and joy, terror and wonder that if she didn't dance, she would burst into flames.

Tam clambered over the rocks towards her, pulled like a moth to a lamp. He tripped and fell, for his eyes were fixed on her. She kept her eyes closed, so she didn't see him coming, and she didn't hear him approaching over the sound of her own song.

Tam drew close. He hid behind a rock, in case she opened her eyes. She was the most wonderful, the most beautiful thing he had ever seen in his life. He had been waiting all his life to meet her, but never known it.

On the sand, close to where she danced, was a sealskin.

Tam stared at the skin. He looked up again at the woman, with her pale skin and chestnut brown hair, dancing naked on the beach at midsummer.

He understood now what she was.

She was a seal-woman. A silkie.

Tam knew a hundred silkie stories; every fisherman did. Some folk believed in them, some folk didn't, and Tam was one of the ones who didn't. But he couldn't deny his own eyes. The woman in front of him was a silkie; a person who wore the skin of a seal and lived out on the sea.

The night passed. The silkie went on dancing. Hours went by and Tam barely noticed. As swiftly as a gannet strikes the sea, he had fallen in love with the silkie woman. Everything she felt, he wanted to feel too. He had to be with her; he had to marry her.

There was a problem, though. A very big problem. She was a silkie. When the sun rose, she would grab her skin, wrap it around her shoulders and dive into the sea. She would be a seal again.

A dark thought stole into Tam's mind.

No, he told himself. He couldn't do that.

But he had to be with her. He would love her like no-one else could, and she would be happy with him. This was the only way to do it. She would thank him for it, in time.

Tam emerged from his hiding place.

He crept from the rocks, onto the sand. Ever so quietly, he circled the silkie woman until he reached the place where her sealskin lay. He picked it up and took it back to his hiding place, stowing it among the rocks.

Tam waited.

Soon, the air brightened. The sky turned crimson and scarlet as the sun rose over the horizon.

The moment it rose, the silkie woman ceased dancing. She opened her eyes and looked for her skin and... it wasn't where she left it. Frantically she searched for it.

She shrieked as Tam leapt upon her.

He wrestled her to the ground. She was strong but he was

stronger. He wrapped his arms around her and threw her over his shoulder. Grabbing her sealskin and putting it under his arm, Tam set off for home as she kicked and punched and screamed.

By the time they reached Tam's house, she had given up screaming and struggling. Tam's mother was out of bed. She was bent over the fireplace, stirring a pot of porridge, when the front door burst open. In came Tam, with a sealskin under one arm and a naked woman over his shoulder.

'What? Who..?'

Tam paid her no notice. He locked the front door behind him and sat the woman down on a chair before the fire. He took a blanket and wrapped it around her.

She stared into the fire.

Tam filled a bowl of porridge and put it into her hands. It fell to the floor.

'Tam, what is going on?'

Tam explained to his mother. She thought it was madness, but he didn't care what she thought.

He didn't go out fishing that day. All day he tended to the silkie woman, bringing her food and drink, telling her all would be well. He told her she would get used to living in a house, and to him.

He only left her to hide away her sealskin.

Tam had a room at the back of the house where he kept his fishing gear. In there was an old sea chest he'd inherited from his father. He locked the skin in the chest, and put the key on a string about his neck.

The summer passed. The silkie woman sat in her chair, staring into the flames of the fire. The look on her face was that of a caged animal. At first she refused all food and drink; but she had to eat and drink, so soon enough she did. Tam sat with her every evening, talking to her, telling her stories, making clothes for her. Whether out of boredom, loneliness or the first stirrings of affection, she began to respond. She started to sit at the table when they had their meals, to use a knife and fork. There were a few books in the house, and Tam read to her. Later he taught her to read. She learnt quickly, reading each book over and over, discussing them with Tam late into the night.

By the time winter came, they were talking and laughing together as if they had known one another for years.

Spring came. The silkie woman had fallen in love with Tam. He married her, and she began to take ill in the mornings.

They had their first child the following winter, a boy. A girl followed the next year, and both children were blessed with health. They grew up never knowing their mother's secret, for after Tam's mother died a few years later, no-one in the world but Tam and his silkie bride knew it.

Tam's wife didn't even want to admit the truth to herself. It was easier to forget her other life; easier to forget that the man she loved had torn her from it, kicking and screaming. Since Tam took her skin, her memories of her life beneath the waves had faded, as had her anger towards Tam. That life was no more than a dream now, her memories as faint as wisps of smoke.

'Tam,' she said to him in bed one night, the first time she joined him there. 'I need you to promise me something.'

'What?'

'Promise me you'll never let me see my sealskin. I know you have it hidden somewhere. You must keep it safe, for if you destroyed it, it would destroy me. But you must, must keep it hidden. For all I love you, and wish to be with you always, I know what will happen if I see my skin.

'I'll touch it. If I touch it, I'll stroke it. If I stroke it, I'll want to put it to my face and smell it. If that happens, nothing on earth, sea or sky will keep me from running to the water. I would dive beneath the waves, and never come back to you.'

Tam took her words seriously. He always kept the key on the string around his neck, or buried deep in his pockets.

Word went about North Berwick one summer that there would be a fair at the kirk. The town was buzzing with excitement. There would be jugglers and tumblers, singers and players, and traders selling all manner of things.

The morning of the fair came. Tam and his wife were sitting at the table, eating their breakfast while the children danced around the room, too excited to eat.

'Are we going yet, Daddy? Mummy, can we go now?'

'I'm ready,' said Tam, finishing his porridge. 'Mum, are you ready?'

'No,' she said. 'I've still got the washing to take in.'

'Oh, but Mum...'

'You all go,' said Tam's wife. 'It won't take me long, and I'd like to know everything is done before I leave. Go on, I'll see you there.'

Tam kissed her on her cheek and left, the children running ahead of him.

After clearing up the breakfast dishes, Tam's wife went out to the garden with the washing basket. She lifted Tam's trousers off the line and something fell from his pocket onto the grass.

She knelt down and picked it up.

It was a key.

She looked at it for a long time.

Two voices whispered in her mind. One said, *put it back in his pocket. Leave the house now. Join your family and forget this ever happened.*

The other said, *it wouldn't hurt to look. Just one look, for old time's sake.*

She turned around and went back into the house.

Through the hall she walked. She opened the door to Tam's fishing room.

It was dark in there, the salty smell of the ocean thick in the air. Faint light entered through one dusty window. At the back of the room was an old sea chest.

She walked over to it, knelt down and put the key in the lock.

She turned the key. The lock clicked open.

Warnings screamed in her mind as she opened the chest.

Within it was her skin.

She shuddered. So many forgotten things came flooding back. Her people, her cave, the surging sea beneath her...

It was enough to look. She should close the chest now.

But she didn't.

She reached out and touched it. Stroked it.

Her fingers gripped it tightly. Before she could stop herself she buried her face in it, rubbing her brow against it.

Yes, she said to herself. *Yes, this is right. I want this.*

Her children's faces appeared in her mind, as if their spirits were crying out to her; and she almost answered. But in that moment, she breathed in the smell of the skin. The sea's roar filled her ears and filled her mind.

She ran out of the room; out of the house. She ran to the

beach, waded into the water and plunged in, tears streaming down her face.

When Tam and the children arrived home that afternoon, they saw that the door of the house was wide open.

The children went rushing in, shouting 'Mummy, Mummy, look what I bought!'

Tam stood in the garden, staring at the open door.

He felt in his pocket for the missing key.

In that moment, Tam knew he would never see his wife again.

He never did.

His children did, though. They would be walking or playing on the beach, and sometimes they would hear the bark of a seal. They would look out to sea, and there, bobbing on the waves, was a seal. It would see them watching and cry out to them, again and again. It was the saddest sound they ever heard; that and the sound their father made, weeping alone by the fire each night.[1]

---

1. *The silkies (more commonly called selkies, but I prefer silkies) are one of Scotland's most famous legendary races. Seals used to be found in their hundreds of thousands around Scotland's shores, and are still very common today. Many of the stories about silkies involve a romance between a silkie and a human, which rarely ends well.*

   There is an incredible correlation between the silkie stories of Scotland the encantado stories of Amazonia. The encantados (enchanted ones) are pink river-dolphins which can take off their skins to reveal men beneath, who turn up at parties to seduce human women.

Strangely, Scotland's seas are home to many dolphins, yet we seem to have no folklore about them. I bring Scotland's dolphins, as well as the silkies, into my novel, The Shattering Sea.

9

THE WELL AT WORLD'S END

Edinburgh Castle was once home to the King and Queen of Scotland, who had two daughters. One was the King's daughter by his first Queen, who had died when her little girl was young. She was known as the King's Daughter. The other girl was the new Queen's daughter; she was known as the Queen's Daughter.

The King's Daughter was a charming girl, kind and polite to everyone she met. When the servants served her food at the banqueting table, she would tell them it was delicious, even if it was revolting. When she rode in her carriage through the streets of Edinburgh, and the common folk waved and shouted hello to her, she would wave back and throw gold coins.

The Queen's Daughter couldn't have been more different. She was short-tempered, spiteful and cruel. If she didn't like her dinner, she would have the cook's head chopped off, right there at the feasting table. When she rode in a carriage through the streets of Edinburgh, she would lean out of the window and spit on her subjects.

Everyone loved the King's Daughter, and everyone hated the Queen's Daughter. The Queen was aware of this, and it infuriated her. She began to think that life would be better if the King's Daughter wasn't around; if the King's Daughter was dead.

Of course, she couldn't just put a sword through the girl herself. She would need to be above suspicion. What could she do? She paced her chambers and racked her mind until one day she had an idea. Laughing, she sent a servant to fetch the King's Daughter.

'Yes, mother?' said the King's Daughter when she arrived.

'I have a job for you to do,' said the Queen, thrusting a bottle into the girl's hands. 'Take this bottle to the well at World's End and fetch me some water.'

'Yes, Mother. Where exactly is this well?'

'I just told you; it's at the end of the world. Go!'

The King's Daughter ran off to prepare for her journey. She put on some stout boots, donned a thick travelling cloak and filled her purse with gold and silver coins. She left the castle, left the city and set out into the world.

The Princess enjoyed the first days of her journey. The sun shone each day, and she slept in the finest rooms at the finest inns. She met new people, saw new places and wished to keep walking forever. Every day, she walked in the same direction, knowing that eventually she would reach World's End.

Overseas and through foreign kingdoms she went, as the weeks and months rolled by. The journey began to take its toll on her. She no longer had enough coin to sleep in lavish rooms. When her purse grew light, she began to work a day or a week in places. The Princess swept floors, washed dishes and picked potatoes.

When she finally ran out of coin, she stopped sleeping in inns altogether. She slept in the forest and washed in the river; she begged and even stole for food. Her feet were bare, she was bone-thin and her cloak and clothes were ragged. By now, she was out near the edge of the world, where all people and places are wild.

Finally, after years of travel, she arrived at the last forest in the world. Beneath the vast trees she ran, flitting from shadow to shadow, fearful of the strange creatures that lurked there.

After many days, she reached the far edge of the forest. Beyond it was a misty moor covered in bramble bushes, and tied to the last tree in the world was a scruffy white pony. Ribs poked through its scabby skin and it smelt of rotten turnips.

The pony saw the King's Daughter approaching. It brayed and sang to her.

Free me, free me,
My bonny maiden,
For I haven't been free,
Seven years and a day

'Of course I'll free you,' said the King's Daughter. She untied the rope from around the pony's neck.

'Thank you,' said the pony. 'Since you have freed me, I will carry you over the Moor of Sharp Thorns.'

The King's Daughter climbed onto the pony's back, and he raced off over the moor. Bramble bushes covered every inch of the ground. Her legs would have been torn to ribbons, but the pony's tough legs were unscathed.

They arrived at the far end of the moor. The King's Daughter threw her fist in the air, whooped and howled.

She had reached the very end of the world.

In front of her was a wall of darkness and stars. The stony ground ended just before it. She went to the edge and looked over, seeing nothing but darkness and stars below. This was the very, very edge of the world.

The King's Daughter wanted to walk along the edge and

take a look around. But she had a job to do, and nearby, right at the edge of the world, was a well.

She walked to the well, put her hands on the rim and looked in.

In a bucket at the bottom were three green, slimy, scaly men's heads.

All at once, the heads opened their eyes. They looked at the Princess, grinned and sang to her.

Clean us, clean us,
My bonny maiden,
For we haven't been clean
Seven years and a day

'No problem,' said the King's Daughter. She hauled up the bucket and placed it on the edge of the well. One by one, she took the heads and scrubbed them with the edge of her cloak, until they glistened in the light of the stars.

The heads looked at each other. They seemed pleased.

'Wish, brother, what do you wish?' they said in chorus.

'I wish,' said the first head, 'that if she were bonny before, she'll be ten times bonnier now.'

'Oh, thank you, but I'm not bonny...'

Instantly, she was ten times bonnier than she had been before.

'Wish, brother, what do you wish?' the heads said in chorus.

'I wish,' said the second head, 'that every time she touches her hair, gold and silver coins come tumbling out of it.'

'Oh, there's no need for that...' she said, touching her straggly, knotted hair. The moment she touched it, gold and silver coins fell from it onto the ground.

'Thank you!' said the King's Daughter, gathering up the coins.

'Wish, brother, what do you wish?' the heads said in chorus once more.

'I wish,' said the third head, 'that every time she opens her mouth, a slice of cake comes falling out of it.'

'Really? Cake?' said the Princess. Out of her mouth fell a slice of cake. She caught it, ate it and said, 'Thank you, that was delicious!' As soon as she did so, another slice fell out. She ate that, and another, and another. It had been a long time since she had eaten cake.

Once she had finished eating, she filled her bottle with water, put the men's heads back in the basket and lowered it into the well again. She climbed onto the pony, rode it back over the moor and tied it to its tree, before setting off home.

It had taken her years to reach the end of the world; it took her years to return. At long last, she arrived in Edinburgh. She passed through the Netherbow Gate into the city, walked up the Royal Mile to Edinburgh Castle and was admitted to her mother's chambers.

'Here's the water you asked for,' she said to her mother.

The Queen stared at the Princess as if she were a ghost. The girl had been gone for over seven years. The Queen had assumed that she was dead. Not only was she alive; she was ten times bonnier than before, with coins pouring from her hair and cake falling from her mouth.

This wouldn't do. The Queen took the bottle and dismissed the King's Daughter. She racked her brains until finally an idea struck her.

The Queen sent for her own daughter.

'What do you want?' said the Queen's Daughter when she arrived.

'Take this bottle to the well at World's End and fetch me some water, now!' said her mother.

The Queen's Daughter refused, but her mother beat her and threatened her until she acquiesced. Soon she was on the road, stout boots on her feet and coins jingling in her purse.

Like her sister, the Queen's Daughter travelled for weeks, months and years. Like her sister, she started off sleeping in luxurious inns, and ended up sleeping in ditches and haylofts. She grew thin and wild-eyed, her boots fell apart and if you had seen her on the road, you would have hidden behind a tree until she passed.

It took a long time, but by putting one foot in front of the other, she finally reached the last tree in the world. Tied to it, just as before, was the mangy white pony. Just as before, it sang its song.

Free me, free me,
My bonny maiden,
For I haven't been free,
Seven years and a day

The Queen's Daughter couldn't believe what she was hearing.

'I'm not freeing you, you filthy ragamuffin of a pony!' she said.

'Very well,' said the pony. 'Be on your way.'

The Queen's Daughter went on her way, which led over the Moor of Sharp Thorns. She screamed and cried the entire way, for a thousand thorns tore at her cloak and skirt and skin. By the time she reached the other side, she had no cloak left, no skirt and no skin; her legs had been stripped to flesh and bone.

She was in a foul mood now; but she smiled when she saw the well before her.

The Queen's Daughter approached the well. She peered into its depths. There was the bucket, and in the bucket were three green, slimy, scaly men's heads.

All at once, their eyes opened. All at once, they grinned and sang.

> Clean us, clean us,
> My bonny maiden,
> For we haven't been clean
> Seven years and a day

'Clean you? Clean you? If I lived to be a thousand years old, I wouldn't clean you, you revolting men's heads!'

The heads looked at each other. They seemed pleased.

'Wish, brother, what do you wish?' they said in chorus.

'I wish,' said the first head, 'that if she were ugly before, she'll be ten times uglier now.'

The Queen's Daughter was a pretty girl, but she had been made ugly through years of sneering and glaring. Now, her face contorted and twisted until it looked like it had been scrubbed with rocks.

'How dare you–'

'Wish, brother, what do you wish?' the heads said in chorus.

'I wish,' said the second head, 'that every time she touches her hair, fleas and flies come leaping out of it.'

'They certainly will not–' as she spoke, the Queen's Daughter put her hand to her hair. A cloud of fleas and flies swarmed out of it and jumped and buzzed around her head.

'You impudent men's heads! I order you to–'

'Wish, brother, what do you wish?'

'I wish,' said the third head, 'that every time she opens her mouth, she's sick.'

'I will not–' the Queen's Daughter didn't get any further. A jet of vomit erupted from her mouth.

'I demand that you stop this–' she vomited again. She went on vomiting until she had nothing left in her.

The Queen's Daughter didn't bother collecting the water. She turned around and set off home, over the Moor of Sharp Thorns and across the world. Days and weeks, month and years passed before she found herself standing before her mother once more.

The Queen was not especially pleased to see her daughter. The Princess was supposed to come back as a beautiful young woman, showering coins and cake wherever she went. Instead, she had returned with skinned legs, fleas and flies buzzing about her, a hideous face and an endless stream of vomit leaving her lips.

A few years later, the King's Daughter married a handsome prince. She became a queen, and she and her husband ruled over their subjects wisely and benevolently. The Queen's Daughter married the prince of a midden heap. She lived the rest of her life on the midden heap, and ate fleas, flies and vomit every day.[1]

---

1. *This is a story I have told countless times in schools, where it always goes down riotously well. If telling it to children, I would recommend asking them to imagine creatures that might live in the forest at the edge of the world, and to imagine what the end of the world might look like before you describe it.*

   There is a related story in which the princess finds a frog in the well, who asks him to chop off her head, and when she does so, he becomes a handsome prince. Asking someone to chop your head off is much more common in folklore than in modern life.

10

A CLOSE TONGUE

This is a story from Orkney, an archipelago of islands off the Northeast coast of Scotland. Orkney is a unique place, where the ancient past is never far away, and is home to some of Scotland's most wonderful stories. Many of those stories concern the finfolk.

The finfolk are a mysterious race of people, who live on a hidden island called Hildaland in summer before retiring to the undersea city of Finfolkaheim in winter. They are said to row boats with no sails, and can row all the way to Iceland with seven strokes of an oar. Their bodies are covered in fins, which they can disguise with the aid of magic, so that they appear as tall, dark men.

There once lived on the Isle of Sanday a man named Tam Scott. Tam had a friend, Willy, and the two of them worked together, running a ferry from Sanday to Kirkwall on the mainland. When Orcadians say the mainland, they are referring to the main island in Orkney, not to Scotland, which some see as quite a separate country.

Every year at Lammas, a fair was held at Kirkwall. People came from all over Orkney, and as far away as Sutherland and Shetland, to buy, sell and enjoy the festivities. Everybody had been looking forward to the fair for weeks, and finally, the day had come.

The sky was grey and a good wind was blowing as Tam and Willy ushered their passengers onto the ferry. They left the harbour and set off, the boat full of people laughing and joking, and Tam smiled and laughed as he steered the boat.

They reached Kirkwall and docked in the harbour. Everybody rushed off the boat in the direction of St Magnus' Cathedral, where stalls would be set up and traders would be trading.

'I'm not one for haggling with traders,' said Willy to Tam. 'I think I'll go and have a drink.'

'Alright,' said Tam, 'I'll see you back at the boat, if not before.'

Tam wandered alone through the fair, chatting with acquaintances he met and catching up on the news. He was thinking of going for a cog of ale himself when someone tapped him on the shoulder.

Tam turned around. Standing there was a tall, dark-haired, dark-eyed man.

'You're Tam Scott?' asked the stranger.

'Yes,' said Tam. 'Do I know you?'

'You have a ferry?' asked the stranger.

'I do, aye.'

'Good. I want to buy your services, Tam. I need to get to one of the North Isles. Can you do that?'

'Of course,' said Tam. It was still morning; his passengers wouldn't be returning to Sanday until the evening. 'I'll need to fetch Willy. We'll meet you down at the dock.'

'Very well,' said the stranger.

Tam made his way to the Anchor, Willy's favourite watering hole. When he arrived, Willy wasn't inside the pub.

He was outside it, lying in the gutter.

Tam tried to wake him, to no avail. Though Willy was a good seaman, he was over-fond of ale, and nothing on earth could wake him when he passed out drunk.

Cursing, Tam turned around and headed towards the harbour. He would just have to go without Willy and hope he didn't run into trouble.

Tam reached the harbour and looked about for the stranger. It wasn't hard to spot him. The stranger stood on the harbour with a cow at his side.

The cow was blue. As blue as the summer sky.

'Are you ready, Tam?' asked the stranger as Tam approached.

'I'm ready, yes, it'll just be me,' said Tam, trying not to stare at the cow. 'Now, we'll need to load the cow onto the boat...'

Before Tam could say any more, the stranger put him arm beneath the cow's belly and hoisted it up onto his shoulder. He stepped onto the ferry and set it down.

'Don't just stand there staring, Tam! Lets get moving!'

'...Yes, of course,' said Tam. He hopped in, untied the rope and rowed them out of the harbour.

Out onto the open sea they went. Seals bobbed on the surface while gulls swooped overhead.

'Is it Shapinsay you're going to?' asked Tam.

'East of Shapinsay,' said the stranger, not looking at Tam but out to sea.

He must be going to Stronsay, Tam thought. He steered towards Stronsay, which was the next island east of Shapinsay.

As they sailed along, Tam thought to make conversation to pass the time. He was very curious about this stranger and his blue cow.

'That's some cow you've got there,' he said. 'I've never seen its like. How did you come by it?'

The stranger turned and looked at Tam. 'A close tongue keeps a safe head,' he said in a low voice.

Tam shivered. He focussed on steering the boat.

Soon, it was time to steer towards Stronsay.

'Are you going to Stronsay?' he asked.

'East of Stronsay,' said the stranger.

Sanday it is then, thought Tam.

They sailed in silence, the stranger staring out to sea. Tam decided to try for conversation again.

'Do you have family on Sanday? I'm from Sanday myself...'

The stranger fixed Tam with another icy glare.

'A close tongue keeps a safe head,' he said.

Tam shook his head and gave up on conversation.

It was time to steer towards the harbour at Sanday. Tam began to turn his boat when the stranger said, 'East of Sanday.'

'East of Sanday?' said Tam. 'East of Sanday? I'm not going east of Sanday! Why, there isn't anything east of Sanday except open sea all the way to Norway, and my ferry wasn't made for crossing to Norway...'

Once more, the the stranger fixed his gaze on Tam.

'East of Sanday,' he said. He said it quietly this time, in a way that made Tam wish he had never laid eyes on the stranger.

Tam turned the ferry east.

The sea grew rough and choppy. Water sloshed onto the deck and Tam was terrified.

'We need to turn around!' said Tam.

The stranger shook his head, still looking out east, seemingly unconcerned. As Tam watched, he raised his hand and waved it in the air while speaking a language Tam had never heard.

A mist blew in. Tam couldn't see three feet in any direction.

'We're doomed,' said Tam. 'Doomed...'

The stranger spoke strange words again. At once, the sea calmed. The mist cleared.

Tam couldn't believe his eyes.

The sky was a brilliant blue. Beneath them, the sea was a sheet of glass. Before them was an island, and it was the most beautiful island Tam had ever seen. Golden corn waved in the breeze on little hills, and the fields were dotted with herds of blue cows. The sand on the beach was as white as polished bone, the water surrounding it crystal-clear.

As Tam stared, he noticed women with fish-tails singing on rocks near the beach. Seeing Tam, they called out to him and slipped into the water, swimming towards him at breathtaking speed.

'I'll need to blindfold you, Tam,' said the stranger. 'This is not for your eyes to see.'

The stranger produced a strip of cloth from his pocket, and Tam allowed himself to be blindfolded. He understood now who the stranger was. He was a finman, and the island was Hildaland, the legendary vanishing island of the finfolk.

Tam heard sweet singing around him as the mermaids emerged from the water. They invited him to join them in the water and to kiss them.

'There'll be none of that,' shouted the finman. 'He has a wife and children back on Sanday.'

The mermaids hissed, snarled and shrieked at Tam before swimming away.

Tam sat still as the finman guided the boat into the harbour. He felt the boat rock as the stranger lifted the cow out onto the shore.

'Now then, Tam,' said the finman. 'You've done a good job, and here's your payment.' He put a heavy bag into Tam's hands. 'I'll turn around the boat now. When you feel the wind blowing, take off your blindfold, but not before.'

Tam nodded. He felt the stranger climb out of the boat, turn it around and push it off.

Tam's ferry floated out to sea. He shivered as the air cooled, and when the wind began to blow, he took off his blindfold.

Tam was south of Shapinsay. The sky was grey, just as it had been before. He shook his head. Had he been imagining things?

No. He hadn't. For in his hands was the bag the finman had given him. He looked inside and saw that it was full of gold coins. Tam was rich.

He guided the boat back to Kirkwall. Willy had sobered up by this point, and they took their passengers back to Sanday. Once there, Tam went to the inn at the harbour and sat down at the bar.

'Drinks for everyone, on me!' he said, thumping the bag down on the bar.

'Skies above,' said the barman. 'Where did you get all that money?'

Tam smiled. 'From a finman,' he said.

Everyone gathered round to listen as Tam told his tale. Some believed him and some didn't; but everyone was willing to accept drinks from him as they listened. The occupants of the inn drank at Tam's pleasure until closing time.

The next evening, he was back in the inn. More folk had come to hear his tale, and he treated them all. Tam had never had coin to spare before. It felt good to share his wealth around, to show folk how well he'd done for himself.

Eventually, everyone had heard Tam's tale, but that didn't stop him from telling it. He passed every evening in that inn or another, buying drinks for anyone who would listen to him. By the end of the evening he would be swearing and cursing as men mocked his story of blue cows and finmen.

'Where did I get this then, eh?' he would ask, jingling his bag of coins, which was growing steadily lighter.

Eventually no-one would speak to Tam, not even if he bought them drinks. His wife and children ignored him. He grew sullen and miserable. When the Lammas fair came around the next year, he spoke to no-one as he steered the boat over to Kirkwall.

Tam drank alone in the Anchor for a while before wandering down the street towards the cathedral. As he walked, he saw someone familiar.

It was the finman.

He was facing away from Tam, strolling down the street, but Tam was sure it was him. He ran after the finman and tapped him on the shoulder.

'It's yourself!' said Tam. 'I thought it was you there!'

The finman stared at Tam. 'You see me?' he said.

'Aye,' said Tam with a grin. 'It's been a while. How have you been? Did everything work out with that cow?'

'You see me?' said the finman again, reaching into his pocket.

'Aye, of course I see you,' said Tam.

'Well don't you worry, Tam,' said the finman. As he spoke, he took a tiny wooden box from his pocket and held it up in front of Tam. He opened it up; it was full of a fine powder.

'You see me now,' he said, 'but you won't see me again.'

The finman blew sharply on the powder. Tam screamed as it stung his eyes.

The finman spoke the truth. Tam never saw him again. In fact, Tam never saw anything again. From that moment until his dying day, Tam Scott was completely blind.[1]

---

1. *I heard this story from Tom Muir, an Orcadian storyteller and historian who has done a huge amount of work to preserve Orkney's folklore. Tam's descent into drunkenness after the incident is my own addition to the story. The finmen hold a particular fascination for me, and are central to* The Shattering Sea. *You can hear me telling* A Close Tongue *on House of Legends Podcast.*

The fairy ointment motif is another common folklore motif, in which a fairy or otherworld creature asks a human to do a job for them, and in the process, accidentally gifts them with them the ability to see the otherworld. You can hear an Irish story of this kind told by Maria Gillen on House of Legends Podcast.

11

LADY ODIVERE

Some of these stories reach back to Scotland's ancient past, while others took place only a few lifetimes ago. This tale takes us back a thousand years, to a time of Vikings, crusaders and holy wars.

Orkney was in the hands of the Northmen, who had crossed from Scandinavia in their longships and conquered the islands. They had left their raiding ways behind them, and now lived as lords and earls, farmers and fishermen.

Among them were a lord and his wife who both died young, ravaged by the same sickness. They left behind their daughter Estrid, who inherited their hall and all their servants with it. Estrid grew up with wealth and comfort, yet without a parent's guidance or love.

Estrid was in love with the sea. The land seemed lifeless

to her, compared to the restless, turbulent ocean. She would take herself off to the cliffs and coves to swim all day and, best of all, to dive. Estrid never felt more free than when she plunged like a gannet into the cold, salty water.

Years passed. Estrid could no longer be called a girl. She was a young woman, with sea-blue eyes, a proud, Viking bearing and all her parents' wealth at her command.

Suitors were not slow to appear. They strutted into her hall full of pomp and pride, boasting of battles and conquests. None of them stirred her heart. For all their tales of daring, they were as dead to her as the stones beneath her feet. She wanted a man whose blood hummed with life, the way a violin string shivers when the bow strikes.

Her prayers were answered.

Into Estrid's hall, one warm summer's evening, walked a man named Lord Odivere.

Odivere was a colossal man, who didn't walk so much as prowl. He was as big as a bear yet as lithe as cat; his eyes burned like the heart of the sun. His sword was the length of other men's spears, and his voice rang out like a trumpet's cry.

Estrid welcomed Odivere and dined with him. He frightened her, but he amused her too. Odivere brought musicians in his retinue, and come midnight, he had her twirling and leaping around the hall. He laughed his booming laugh as he lifted her into the air; he purred with satisfaction as she pressed in close to him, throwing her head back to laugh, exhilarating in the music. Later, as they drank by the fire and he told tales of his deeds, she kept getting the feeling that he had done far more than he claimed, not less.

The sun had already risen when Estrid finally went to bed. Staring up at the ceiling, she asked herself: could she love such a man?

Estrid was no fool. There was artfulness in Odivere's dancing, his tales, his singing. The charms he wove on her were surely well-practiced. A glint of cruelty hid in his eyes and his laughter. His very presence thrilled her and frightened her; her wisdom warned her away from him.

And yet, she wanted him. She wanted him so badly that she knew she wouldn't say no to him. It was as if she were under a spell, some strange intoxication, which drowned out all careful voices.

In truth, she was.

Odivere had heard many tales of Estrid, the blue-eyed beauty who disdained all suitors. Rather than leave his courting of her to chance, he took steps to ensure she would be his bride.

Before visiting Estrid's hall, Odivere crossed the sea to Norway. In a pagan temple deep in the forest, he drew his own blood and took Odin's oath. He swore to the Allfather that he would pay any price for Estrid's hand.

Before leaving her hall, Odivere asked Estrid to marry him. She agreed, and went to live in his castle.

Odivere was infatuated with his bride. He gave all his

ceaseless energy to her, and soon found that in running and swimming, drinking and laughing, singing and tale-telling, she was his match. They both wished to drink deep of the cup of life, day and night, and each was overjoyed to find another like themselves.

Yet, there are some pleasures an island cannot offer. Word reached Odivere that a call had gone out to fight the pagan hordes in the Holy Land. Odivere worshipped Odin and the gods of his ancestors, but he followed Christ too, especially when there was slaughter to be done in his name.

Battle-hunger awakened in Odivere. Once awakened, only blood could quench it.

He told his wife he would be leaving. She wept, but didn't try to stop him. Estrid knew it would be easier to stop the sun from setting than to keep her husband from the battlefield. Days later, she stood alone on the beach as she watched his ship depart.

Seasons passed, summer sun and winter snow. Lady Odivere yearned for her husband in a way she had never yearned for anyone, not even her parents. She had never been blind to Odivere's faults. The servants were happier now that he was gone; they no longer had to fear his black tempers. Those same tempers had never scared her. She knew how to deflect them, and in a strange way they thrilled her.

Every day, every hour with her husband had been different, never knowing what mood or desire would take him next. Now, every day was the same. She ate, sang and slept alone. She walked on the windy clifftops alone.

After a year had passed, she began to look out to sea, searching the horizon for ships. He had to come home someday, so why not that day? With each day that passed, she grew more certain that he would be home soon. It became her way of life, to dress in fine clothes and sit on the shore, watching and waiting for him. To pass the time, she sang his favourite songs. In her mind, the wind would carry her voice to him, and he would hear it and urge the rowers on.

He never came.

Winter arrived; the fifth winter since he left. It swept over the islands, shrieking and howling in an endless assault of storms. Everyone from earls to farmers stayed within their homes, praying that their walls wouldn't topple on their heads.

On a night in the depths of that winter, a knock sounded on Odivere's door.

Again and again the knocker knocked, until the bars were lifted and a servant's face appeared to scrutinise the visitor.

'Who comes knocking at such an hour, on such a night?'

'One with word of Lord Odivere.'

The servant's eyes widened. He hurried the visitor inside and went to fetch his mistress.

Taking off his cloak, the visitor looked around him. The

hall was richly furnished, with a long fire-pit running down the centre and lines of shields and spears upon the walls.

A door at the rear of the hall opened. In walked Lady Odivere.

She stared at her visitor. The man had silky brown hair and deathly-pale skin. He had a lithe, slender form and bright brown eyes, which shone when he saw her. On his finger he wore a gold ring.

She knew him.

Before Odivere came to her door, back when she was still fending off suitors, Estrid had gone to the beach one night for a midnight swim. She dived from a cliff, and when she emerged from the water, she saw a man atop the cliff, right where she had stood. He grinned at her and dived, spinning and somersaulting in ways she had never thought possible.

'Who are you?' she asked him when he surfaced. He had brown hair, bright, brown eyes and a mischievous smile.

'Let us put names aside,' he said, 'and dive instead.'

'If you wish,' said Estrid.

They dived together for hours, the stranger teaching her all his tricks, which she quickly learned. They raced one another, wrestled and made love on the moonlit sand.

'Will I see you here again?' she asked as they lay wrapped in one another's arms.

'Don't let tomorrow intrude upon today,' he said.

'If you wish,' said Estrid, unaware that many moons would ride the sky before they met again.

'I apologise for the intrusion, Lady Odivere,' said her visitor with a glance towards the servant, 'especially since we are not known to one another. Yet I bring word of your husband, and I thought you would rather have it sooner than later.'

'You were right. Please, sit, and we shall eat and talk.'

Servants heated food while they sat down across from one another. It was whispered in the kitchens that Lady Odivere had a strange manner with this man. She seemed more interested in him than the news he bore.

'So,' said Lady Odivere after the time for pleasantries had passed, 'what would you tell me of my husband?'

'Let me begin at the beginning,' said her visitor.

'I often sail to Norway to trade. Not along ago, I was in a shoreside tavern in Bergen when I met a man I once traded with, many years ago.

'We greeted one another and fell to drinking and talking. He told me that his path had taken him to Micklegard, and while there he met a lord from Orkney, whose name was Odivere.

'Though I have not met your husband, I knew him by reputation. I asked after him. My friend told me that Odivere had fought long and well against the pagan armies, winning many spoils. He had turned for home, but stopped in Micklegard and tarried there. Many Northmen are in that city, you will know, that is said to outshine any other beneath the sun.

'So Odivere remained there,' he went on. 'Ladies shrieked, night after night, at his tales of battle; they clamoured for his songs. My friends told me that Odivere unsheathed his sword many times, on the battlefield and off of it.'

The visitor watched Estrid's face carefully. When she did not respond, he went on, recounting every word, every tale of Odivere that his friend had shared. As he went on, he made it ever more clear which delights Odivere enjoyed most in Micklegard.

One servant remained. He gave a pointed yawn. Lady Odivere turned and said, 'Leave us.'

The servant left them together.

'Why have you come here?' said Lady Odivere. 'Does it amuse you to hurt me?'

'I come for the same reason I first came to you, so many moons ago,' said her visitor. 'Because I love you. If Odivere breaks faith with you, why not break faith with him?'

'You claim my husband is unfaithful. Perhaps it is true; perhaps it is all lies. Lord Odivere has given me a home, his name and his company. You lay with me and disappeared; you never even gave me your name! Why should I trust you?'

He answered by kissing her. She turned away from him at first; but soon she was kissing him back. They lay down together on wolfskins by the fire.

Lady Odivere awoke in her bed. Her visitor was gone.

She spoke nothing of him; the servants didn't ask after him. He was not to be forgotten, though. Lady Odivere was pregnant.

She pleaded with the servants not to speak of her condition. Since she had always been a good mistress, and since they pitied her for all her years left alone, they did as she asked. Yet she had no joy. Her days and nights were as lonely as always. She gave birth to a boy, held him tightly to her breast and kissed him. Her heart remained as cold and grey as the Orkney sky.

The boy was born in the autumn. In the middle of winter, the child's father came to Estrid's door again.

'You cannot remain as you are,' he said. 'Sooner or later, your husband will return. I fear for our son's safety, if Odivere finds him here. Come away with me.'

'I don't want to go anywhere with you! I don't want you! I want my husband,' said Estrid. 'He is a good man. He will come home to me.'

'And what will he say, when he sees you with a child?'

'Are you afraid that he will come after you? I wouldn't worry,' she said. 'How can he, when I don't know your name?'

'My name,' he said, 'is Sam Imravoe.'

Estrid was shocked. After all these years, he had finally given her his name. He spoke as if he were giving his very soul into her keeping.

'I feared to tell you the truth,' he continued. 'I am Sam Imravoe, and I am no man. I am a silkie; the King of Sula Skerry.'

'You... you could have told me,' said Lady Odivere.

'Would you have come there to live with me, never to be among your own kind again?'

She hesitated.

'We will never know. But I know that when you husband returns, he will seize our son and dash out his brains.

'There is only one thing to do. I shall return in six months, at midsummer, and you must give our son to me. I will take him to Sula Skerry, and he will be safe there.'

Estrid refused, screaming at Sam that she and her son would never be parted. But she knew he was right. After six more miserable months, when Sam came to the castle, she agreed to give the child to him. She put a gold chain around the boy's neck, one that her husband had given her.

Estrid's child was gone. Grief took her and clasped her tightly, each day more sorrowful than the last. Days, nights and months passed without her noticing.

Until the day Odivere returned to her.

Servants hammered on her door with the news. Lord Odivere's sails had been spotted. Estrid rushed to see for herself. Yes, it was his ship. As if awakening from an age-long sleep, she rushed back and forth through the castle, not knowing whether to feel happy or terrified.

In through the gates strode Odivere.

'Estrid!' he cried, seeing his wife. He picked her up, twirled her around and kissed her. She laughed, her laughter full of joy and fear.

'I have missed you so,' she said.

'And I you. Now, we shall make up for all these lost years.'

He ordered the servants to see to his things and make his men comfortable, before carrying his wife upstairs to bed.

The following days and nights were passed at the feasting table. Odivere and his retinue ate, drank and told stories of their exploits in the Holy Land.

Lady Odivere ate, drank and listened to their talk. She woke each morning in her husband's arms. At first it felt like a dream to have him returned to her, but she got used to it, and her years without him began to feel like a dream. He showered her with gifts and praise, and she began to doubt what Sam Imravoe had told her. What if it had all been lies?

Yet all too soon, she sensed a change in her husband. His

eyes flicked back and forth across the hall as songs were sung. He was always refilling his cup or sloshing the ale around in it, peering into the dark liquid as if expecting to see mysteries revealed there. Scarcely three weeks had her husband been home, and already he was restless.

One evening he stood up at the table. 'We will grow weak by tarrying at the fireside too long,' he said. 'Idleness does a man no good. Tomorrow, we shall rise early and hunt the otter.'

The men cheered. Odivere sat down looking satisfied.

Before the sun was up the next day, they had gathered to dress and arm themselves for the hunt. Spears in hand, they set off on foot down the shore.

Otters elude all but the most patient of hunters. Odivere had never been patient. He and his men arrived at the beach where otters were often sighted and lay down in the dune-grass to wait. The wind harried them and before long Odivere grew irritable. 'We must have missed the wretched beasts,' he grumbled. 'I said we should have left earlier.'

He stood and shouted at his men that the hunt was over. There was some complaining, as many of the men disputed Odivere's judgement; but none would argue with him.

They set off home in a black mood. As they walked down the shore, they startled a seal pup. It wriggled down the sand in front of them, racing for the water. With a savage snarl, Odivere drew back his spear and cast it at the pup. His aim was true, and he skewered it right through.

The men laughed and cheered; but their cheering soon died. Odivere knelt down over the corpse and took a fine gold chain from the pup's neck.

He knew that chain. He had given it to his wife.

Odivere stormed in through the gates of his castle.

'Estrid! Come here!'

Lady Odivere entered the courtyard. She screamed as her husband threw the dead pup at her feet. It smacked off the flagstones, blood seeping into the cracks.

'I gave you this,' said her husband, holding out the chain. 'You will tell me what it was doing about the neck of a seal pup.'

Lady Odivere paid him no mind. She was on her knees, her arms around the neck of the pup, her cheek pressed against its cheek. Her wretched cries resounded through the hall.

'My baby,' she wailed. 'My baby.'

Everyone save for Lord Odivere departed.

'Your baby,' said Odivere. 'I see now how you spent your days while I was away. I thought you were a good, noble wife. In truth you are a whore–'

'Don't you dare speak of faithlessness with me!' said Estrid, a vengeful glint in her eyes. 'I know how you passed your nights in Micklegard. You bedded every woman in sight, while I was here alone, praying for your safety and return.'

'Lies! I never broke faith with you. When I was on the battlefield, far from home, I faced the pagan hordes with your face in mind. You gave me strength; I survived only so that I could come home to you.

'And what do I get in return? You hold it against me that I do God's work, and you open your legs to beasts.'

'You are the beast–'

Odivere slapped Estrid, knocking her to the ground. He threw her over his shoulder and carried her upstairs; but not to their bedchamber. Odivere took her to a cold tower room, threw her in and locked the door.

Through a narrow window, Lady Odivere watched the days and nights pass. She watched her husband leave one day in his armour, knowing that he set sail for the Thing, the parliament where her fate would be decided.

He returned that evening. By pleading with the servant who collected her chamber pot, she learnt the news. The Thing had met and decided her fate. She would burn at the stake.

Alone in her tower, filthy and shivering, Lady Odivere awaited her fate.

'Sam,' she whispered. 'Sam Imravoe, I wish I had gone

with you.'

Estrid didn't know that Sam had long ago set a watch on her. Back on Sula Skerry, he had learnt of Odivere's return, and all that happened thereafter.

Sam left Sula Skerry. He swam out into the northern ocean, searching the whale-roads where the shepherds of the deep swam. Far out on the ocean, he met a pod of minke whales, who well knew the King of Sula Skerry. They greeted him and listened carefully to his words.

The day of Lady Odivere's burning came. Early in the morning, as people were rising, a cry went out across every island in Orkney.

'Whales! Whales in every cove!'

The islanders rushed to the shore and saw that it was true. Minke, humpbacks and fin whales filled every cove, breaching, blowing and slapping their tails. Everything else was forgotten as men rushed to ready their boats and spears. Meat, fat, blubber, oil and bone would be theirs.

Out to sea they went; but now the whales were moving away. The hunters pursued the whales, yet could not land a single spear. The whales didn't disappear from sight, though. They stayed close, almost as if they were luring the hunters out to sea, away from their homes.

Come evening, every last hunter returned to port defeated and dejected. Not one whale had been caught.

Odivere was among them. He retuned to his castle, slamming his spear down on his table and roaring at his servants to attend him.

No-one came.

Through the corridors he strode, ready to make an example of the first lazy wretch he found.

He found no-one.

Odivere realised something was wrong. He made for the cell where he kept his wife.

He reached her cell.

The door was open.

Lady Odivere was gone.

Odivere never saw his wife again. Estrid went to Sula Skerry with Sam Imravoe and lived there as his Queen.

As for Odivere, he was left alone in his castle. He drank day and night, pounding his bloodied fists against the walls, raging at phantoms by his cold hearth.

He cursed his wife. He cursed his men and his servants, who had all deserted him.

Most of all, he cursed the day he took Odin's oath.[1]

1. *This incredible story has its roots in* The Great Selkie of Sula Skerrie, *a ballad native to Orkney and Shetland. I first heard it told by Ruth Kirkpatrick. While some consider the story to be a forgery by Walter Traill Dennison, Orcadian musicians Kate Fletcher and Corwen Broch have studied it and believe it to be genuine folklore. You can hear their version of the ballad, accompanied by ancient and historical instruments, on their Bandcamp page.*

12

TAMING THE KELPIE

Up in the far Northwest of Scotland, where jagged mountains rise over rain-soaked moors, a young man named John once lived with his parents on their croft. They had a few fields for crops, a herd of milking goats and a horse to drag the plough. John grew up on the croft and never dreamed of going anywhere else. It was a hard life, for crops didn't grow well in the thin soil, but they got by and were happy enough.

As John grew older, his parents grew older. He grew stronger, and they grew weaker and frailer. The crofting work became too much for them, so John took over everything. He did so gratefully, as his parents had cared for him, and he was proud to do the same for them. But they couldn't go on forever, and in time they both died, leaving John alone on the croft.

A few years went by. John worked hard and managed to keep the croft going until tragedy struck. His horse took ill and died.

John was truly alone now, for the horse had been a friend and companion to him. He was frightened, too. He couldn't afford another horse, and how was he to plough the stony fields without it?

Winter came. After winter passed, it would be ploughing season. John kept warm by the fire, telling himself old stories as he sharpened knives and axes. He tried not to worry, but he couldn't help it. One day, he tired of his fire and went out for a walk.

He wandered over the moors and among the lochs. The low winter sun shone out from among the clouds, lighting up the landscape in shades of burnished gold. John was in no mind to appreciate the beauty of it all. What was he going to do? How could he manage without his horse?

He was so caught up in his thoughts that he paid no attention to where he went. Suddenly he came to his senses.

He had come to a loch where no-one ever dared to walk. It was said that a kelpie, a water-horse, lived in the loch. If anyone saw that horse, and got up on its back, it would carry them under the water and drown them.

John stood there, searching the shore for any sign of such a creature. As he stood there, an old woman, a cailleach as they are called in the Gaelic language, came walking past.

'Good afternoon,' she called to him.

'It's not so good,' said John, shaking his head. He reached into his pocket and pulled out a bannock, a cake made from oats that he grew on his croft. 'Would you like a bannock?' he asked her.

'Well, yes, I would,' she said, hirpling over to him and taking the bannock he offered. They ate and talked until the old woman said, 'Well, I'll be getting home before dark, and so should you. But you gave me something, so I'll give you something in return.'

She took from her pocket a woollen shawl. 'You take that,' she said, 'and remember; it can cover more than skin.'

They parted ways. John went home and remained there as the winter deepened. More than ever, he fretted over what he would do come the ploughing season.

One day, he decided to go out walking again. The sky was clear, the air was sharp and the mountains wore their white winter cloak.

John walked without caring where he went. Just as before, he came to the loch where the kelpie was said to live.

This time he walked along its shore, remembering the stories his father used to tell about kelpies. They looked like horses, but with dark, curly beards. A kelpie would walk up to someone on a lochside and lower its hindquarters, looking expectantly at that person, as if offering a ride. When the poor, unsuspecting soul sat upon the kelpie, it would race for the water. The rider would try to leap or climb off, but they would find themselves stuck to the kelpie's back. Into the water they went, never to be seen again.

As John walked, he saw coming towards him the old cailleach.

'Good afternoon, she said. 'It's good to see you again.'

'It's good to see you too.'

'You looked like you were deep in thought, just now,' she said.

'I was only telling myself a story.'

'It's a while since anyone told me a story,' said the old cailleach.

'Well,' said the young man, 'I'll tell you a story.' So he told her the story he had been thinking of, and she told him one, and he told her another.

'Thank you for sharing your stories with me,' she said. 'I'll be getting home now, but let me give you something first.'

From her pocket she took a little pot, which she gave to John. It was full of salt.

'Remember,' she said to him, 'salt can harm as well as heal.'

Midwinter came and went. The wheel of the seasons spun towards spring, and the first snowdrops had broken free when John next went out walking. Patches of melting snow dotted the moor, and the sun felt warm on his face. Winter would be over soon. Ploughing season would come with the spring, and he was without a horse.

Once more, John walked here and there until he found

himself at the edge of the kelpie's loch. He saw the old woman there.

As he drew closer, he saw she was carrying an armful of creels; woven baskets for trapping lobsters. She seemed to be struggling to carry them.

John greeted the old woman and said, 'Where are you taking those creels?'

'I'm taking them home.'

'Would you like some help?'

'Thank you. I would.'

John took a couple of the creels from her. Together they walked over the moors until they came to the little house in which the old woman lived.

'Thank you,' she said. 'You've made my day easier. Now, there's something I'd like to give you.' She bent over an old chest, rummaged around inside and drew out a tangled web of leather and iron. It was a horse's bridle.

'You take that,' she said. 'It can harness more than a horse.'

John walked home.

That night, he sat by his fire, the old woman's gifts laid out before him. The shawl, the pot of salt and the bridle.

He knew what he must do; but he was afraid to do it.

In spite of his fear, John walked to the loch the next day. This time, he had the shawl in his left pocket, the pot of salt in his right pocket and the bridle slung over his shoulder.

He reached the loch. Against a stunted little hawthorn tree he sat, humming tunes to himself, waiting.

The sun sank into the mouth of the west. The birds of night spread their wings across the sky.

John closed his eyes.

He waited.

Drifting in and out of sleep, he was awoken by a gentle whinny.

John opened his eyes. Stood a little way away from him, its dark fur glistening in the moonlight, was the kelpie.

It looked him in the eye and whinnied again. Still looking at John, it lowered its hindquarters.

John got to his feet.

'Oh my,' he said, 'what a beautiful horse you are. Would it be alright if I took a ride on you?'

The kelpie whinnied again. It seemed to nod its head, ever so slightly.

John walked over to it. He stood beside it, ready to climb on.

The kelpie tensed.

John pulled the shawl from his pocket. He threw it over the kelpie's back and leapt atop it.

The kelpie shot to its feet. It tossed its head and neighed at John. The sound was full of anger; for though John was upon its back, the shawl was between him and the kelpie, so he wasn't stuck to it.

The kelpie was furious. It cantered then galloped towards the loch, twisting and bucking as it tried to throw John off. He held on tightly and managed to stay on its back.

The kelpie tried something else.

Before John's eyes, the kelpie's mane turned from hair into a writhing mass of snakes. The snakes reared up, hissing, spitting and striking at John. He leaned back, reached into his pocket and pulled out the pot of salt. John threw the salt all over the snakes and they became hair again.

The kelpie was almost at the water now. It thundered over the grass, determined to take John under the water and drown him. But before they reached the water, John took the bridle from over his shoulder.

The kelpie reared up high, roaring its anger to the night. John threw the bridle over its head and pulled hard.

The bit went between the kelpie's teeth.

The creature instantly calmed. It stood still upon the bank, heaving for breath, waiting for an instruction from John. He had harnessed the kelpie, and it was his to command.

John rode the kelpie home. He put it in his horse's old stable and went to bed.

Spring came. The last of the snow had melted away and the land was humming with life. It was time to plough.

John led the kelpie to his fields and set the plough upon its back. It powered through the fields, breaking up the soil beautifully, and John was overjoyed. He sowed his crop, knowing in his heart that this year's harvest would be a good one.

As for the kelpie?

One day, soon after the ploughing was done, John took it out to the moor at the edge of the croft. He gave it a last affectionate stroke and removed its bridle.

The kelpie didn't hesitate. It shot away from him, over the moor, heading for its underwater home.

How did John get by without it? I don't know. But I think he did the right thing in letting it go. A power like the kelpie can be harnessed for a while, but it can never truly be tamed.[1]

---

1. *I heard this story from Ian Stephen, a fabulous storyteller, author and poet from the Isle of Lewis. I decided to set it in the northwest as there was something in the story that evoked that incredible, primeval landscape for me.*

   The kelpies have returned to Scotland in a striking way. A monument formed of two thirty metre-high horse's heads, named The Kelpies, was completed in 2013 and towers over the land around Falkirk.

13

THE FAIRY LOVER

Many of Scotland's most beautiful places are in the west. Here, you will find the astonishingly beautiful islands of the Inner Hebrides: Coll, Rum, Tiree, Iona and Skye, the Isle of Mists. Even further out, right at the edge of the world, lie the Outer Hebrides, the Isles of Bride, where the goddess herself walks on the white sands.

Lewis is the northernmost island, and Lewis has its own wild west, called Uig. Uig is a landscape that draws some and repels others. Her rocky, marshy, treeless glens are strewn with boulders and lochans, caves and blowholes, standing stones and storm beaches. It's a place of bleak and savage beauty, and it's in Uig that our story takes place.

In the village of Carishader, there once lived a young man. He shared with his parents their blackhouse, tending their cattle, goats and the few crops the ground would give them. He didn't mind the work, but what he liked best was to be away from his home and the warm hearth. Whenever he had time to himself, he would head out to the rocky hills and rainy beaches. There, he could free his mind from the fetters of work, scattering his thoughts upon the wind.

One day, he was out walking among the mountains when a storm blew in, fast and fierce. He made for a place he knew nearby, where heaped boulders offered shelter.

Reaching the rocks, he crawled into the space beneath them.

It was already occupied.

A woman sat there. She was about his age, or so she seemed; a dark-haired beauty with green eyes that pulled him in like whirlpools. Her long, slender fingers caressed a harp, drawing quiet, tender music from it.

'I don't know you,' he said.

'You know me now,' she said. 'Come in out of the rain.'

He sat down and stared at her. 'Where do you bide?' he asked.

'Where do you bide?' she asked him. 'Carishader?'

'Aye,' he said. 'That's fine music you're playing.'

'The music's playing me,' she said.

He didn't know what to make of that, but he stayed and listened as the thunder rumbled and the rain fell. Upon the strings her fingers danced, her dark eyes shone and the young man dreamed he was an eagle, flying proud among an ocean of stars.

Eventually, she said it was time to be leaving. He asked if he could see her again. She said yes, and he asked again where she stayed.

'Let's meet at Mangursta,' she said. She pressed into his hand a stone knife, sharp as death. 'For you to remember me by.'

They parted ways. The young man floated home, the knife in his pocket. He hardly slept until the next time he saw her.

Thus, their courting began. They would meet and walk together, on far-flung beaches or lonely glens, and stop in a cave or at a lochside to sing songs, swap tales or make love on the cold rocks. She was wild in a way he had never known; she loved to run with the red deer, dive into the raging ocean and dance naked in the storms. Love consumed him like a fire set to dry thatch.

It took a while, for love can silence many questions. But he began to wonder why she never introduced him to her people, and why he had kept her a secret from his own. Why she knew so many tales he'd never heard, and why her music had him soaring among the stars. There was a simple answer to all the riddles, yet he didn't want to face it.

They met one day in a high, rainy glen where the red deer roamed. He asked her for the truth.

'Aye,' she said. 'I'm a fairy.'

Now that she'd said it, he could no longer lie to himself. The truth weighed heavily on him as he walked home through the rain.

He was deeply in love with his fairy lover; but she was not alone in stirring his heartstrings. He loved the blackhouse where he had grown up, with its sweet smell of peat smoke and the acrid smells of men and beasts. He loved to run with his lover through the hills in a storm, singing with the shrieking winds; but he also loved the hearth, the click-clack of his mother's needles, the flame of his father's pipe. His family had always worked that croft; its soil was their blood.

His fairy lover could share the wild places with him; but he couldn't bring her home to the blackhouse. She could never be his wife. He knew the tales; such affairs always fell foul, and he wasn't so daft as to think his would be different.

The next time they met, he told her it was over. He turned and walked away from her.

The following days passed as they must. He lay awake at night and sleepwalked through the day; crows of grief tore at his carrion heart. He kept a weather eye open, but never saw her.

One day, he took his fishing boat out to the little islands north of Reef Beach. Coming into shore, he saw her standing on the sand. Something in her eyes turned his blood cold.

He reached for the oars to turn the boat about.

She held up her hand. It clutched a ball of yarn.

She threw it at him, keeping hold of one end. Instinctively, his hand flew up and caught the yarn.

He couldn't let go of it.

She pulled on the yarn, pulling him and his vessel into shore.

Closer and closer he came. Terror grew in him, for her eyes were as cold as the Cailleach's breath.

Closer he came.

As his hull scraped the sand, he remembered what was in his pocket. The stone knife, sharp as death.

He took it out and cut the yarn. She screamed as if he had cut her flesh, while he grabbed his oars and rowed furiously away.

After that, the young man didn't leave Carishader unless he had to. He no longer missed his fairy lover. His heart slowly healed.

One day, a friend of his mother happened to drop by the house. She happened to have her daughter with her, who happened to be about his age. Their mothers made an excuse to leave them alone to talk, and after that, they came by again and again.

This girl didn't play the harp. She had no memory for stories and didn't like to be out in the rain. But she was a hard worker, funny and kind, quick to laugh and quick to forgive. His heart warmed slowly to her, but once warmed, it stayed that way.

They married. She moved into the blackhouse and soon her belly swelled. Her husband put his hand on her belly and imagined roots growing from his feet, through the floor and deep into the earth.

The time came for the baby to be born. The midwife arrived at the house, along with the women who would help her. The young woman who would soon be a mother began to shudder and scream.

Her husband panicked. The midwife told him birth was never easy; he could either calm down or go outside.

He stayed put and kept quiet. Afternoon became evening. Evening became night.

Still, his wife screamed. The look on the midwife's face was different now.

'What's wrong?' he shouted. 'Why aren't you helping her?'

The midwife ordered him out into the night.

It was June, close to midsummer. A clear June night on Lewis is a perpetual dusk. He was able to see clearly as he walked out of the village, away from Carishader and up into the hills. He had to walk. On he went, onwards and upwards through the myriad glens. He walked and walked, stopped to catch his breath; and saw her.

His fairy lover was sitting on a rock, playing her harp, watching him.

'Sit down,' she said.

He sat down beside her.

'You look troubled,' she said.

'I am.'

'Why is that?' she asked.

He hesitated. 'It's... it's one of the goats. She's giving birth, and it's not going well. We're worried we might lose the kid, and her.'

The fairy's slender fingers plucked at the harpstrings.

'I don't think it's a goat that's having trouble giving birth,' she said. 'They're in a field full of pearlwort. I think it's your wife.'

'No,' he said. 'No, no, I don't have a–'

'You needn't worry,' she said with a laugh. 'I was sweet on you once, but I'm not sweet on you now.'

'Aye,' he said. 'It's my wife.'

'Then, for the sake of what we once shared, let me give you this.' She reached into her pocket and took out a length of black rope. 'Take this home. Tie it around your wife's waist, and your wife and bairn will be fine.'

He took it from her and thanked her; she shushed him and said, 'Go, quick!'

He raced like a stag down the hillside. Below him, he soon spied the village; he ran faster and was almost home when he halted.

Words whispered in his mind, too faint to hear. A dreadful suspicion took hold of him.

He looked at the length of rope in his hands.

A boulder stood nearby. He went over to it, tied the rope about it and stood back.

The knot on the rope tightened and split the boulder in two.

His wife and child would die.

His heart shattered; yet as he fell to his knees, words whispered in his mind again. This time he heard them.

'I don't think it's a goat that's having trouble giving birth. They're in a field full of pearlwort.'

Finally, he understood. He dashed to the goats' field, vaulted the fence and grabbed a clump of pearlwort. He ran home, crashed through the door and slipped the pearlwort under his wife's back.

Very soon after that, his baby was born.

It was a boy. The young lad grew up healthy and strong, and his parents loved him fiercely.

As he grew older, the boy often wondered why his parents never went walking on the hills and beaches. Sometimes, when he was alone in the wild places, he heard faint music, and felt hidden eyes upon him.[1]

---

1. *This is one of my absolute favourite stories. It's another one I heard from Ian Stephen, who found in a collection by Bruford and Laing. It's also one of the stories I chose a particular setting for; in this case, Uig. Uig is as powerful landscape as I have found in the world, and is home to Calanais, which for me is the world's most stunning stone circle. The first time I went there, an eagle*

flew circles over the stones as the sun set and a blood moon rose. It's that kind of place.

Pearlwort is believed in Scotland to ward off evil, and some say this is because it was the first plant that Jesus ever stepped on. It is also known as Irish Moss.

14

THE MAKERS OF DREAMS

Long ago, on a bright autumn morning upon the Island of Skye, a group of girls set out to go blae-berry picking. They left their village with their baskets in hand and made for the foothills of the black, sharp-peaked Cuillin mountains.

Though all the girls were laughing, singing and smiling, there was one among them who laughed more joyfully and sang more sweetly than the others, for she gave her heart to every moment that she lived. She was determined to pick the freshest, sharpest and juiciest berries to bring home to her mother. When they reached the foothills of the Cuillins, she stopped singing and focussed on her search.

Picking berries was like hunting to her; she tracked her prey like a hungry wolf. She roved the hills, moving higher and higher, unaware that she could no longer hear laughter or singing. The grass grew thinner beneath her feet, the air colder.

After a long time, she stood and stretched out; then paused.

She looked around.

What had happened? It was morning when they started their search. Now the sun was sinking, her friends were nowhere to be seen and she was... where was she?

She didn't know where she was; but she knew one thing. The foothills of the Cuillins were far below her; she was among the mountains themselves.

She shivered. Wrapping her cloak more tightly about her, she tried to convince herself that all would be well. It wasn't easy. It was evening, and she was alone and lost among the Cuillins. All her life, she had heard tales of these mountains; of giants, dark druids, monsters and cannibals. The stories all agreed on one thing; those who got lost in the Cuillins never found their way out again.

As the dim dusk descended, the wind stirred and blew in a mist from the sea. Within moments she could barely see her hand in front of her face, let alone look for a path. She stood there, helpless, growing colder and colder.

Voices sounded through the mist.

Spectral shapes appeared around her. They surrounded her.

The girl laughed as figures appeared out of the mist. It

was not giants or monsters that surrounded her. It was a herd of deer.

The hinds pressed forward, nosing at her, clearly curious as to what she was doing there.

All of a sudden, they froze. Their ears pricked up.

The hinds set off. Some of them nuzzled and nudged at the girl, making it clear that she was to come with them. She did so, since she had no better plan. They made their sure-footed way through the mist and the gathering dark. The girl followed them as they led her along narrow, winding trails, up and up into the high mountains.

In the day's last hour, the mist cleared. High up among the peaks of the mountains, the hinds led the girl into a hidden glen.

It was the most beautiful glen she had ever seen. Water-falls tumbled down between every peak, little streams criss-crossed the grass and bright flowers adorned the meadows. A rocky buttress looked west over the sea, and she fancied she could see all the way to the edge of the world.

At the far end of the glen was a cave. Firelight flickered within.

The herd led the girl to the cave. She waited outside, peering in as the lead hind entered.

Inside the cave, on seats of stone, sat an old woman and an old man. They weren't simply old; they were ancient, as ancient as the mountains. Between them and their fire was a pool, which they stared into, unblinking.

The lead hind approached the old woman. It spoke to her in soft grunts while the old woman listened, nodding, still staring into the pool.

As the hind went on speaking, the old woman's head shot up. She stared at the girl.

Slowly the old woman got to her feet. She shuffled over to the girl and said, 'What business brings you to the mountains?'

'I was out picking blaeberries, and I got lost,' said the girl. She held out her basket towards the old woman. 'You're welcome to have some. May I stay here for a night?'

The old woman smiled, revealing broken teeth. She turned around and walked over to the old man, who listened as she spoke, nodding, not looking up as he gazed into the pool.

Again, the old woman shuffled over to the girl.

'No,' she said. 'You may not stay here a night.'

The girl's face fell.

'But–'

'You may not stay here for a night. A year and a night, you may stay. I am old, and my work wearies me. Help me with the hinds, and the gathering of herbs, and earn your place by our fire.'

To that, the girl agreed.

~

Time rode by in its spiralling circle. The girl did what was asked, helping the old woman with her work, sharing her life. Not once did the girl ever leave the glen.

Every day, the old woman took a stool and bucket and went out to meet the hinds in the meadows. She sat on the stool, the hinds came to her and she milked them. Once the bucket was full, she carried it back to her cave.

Later in the day, she walked through the glen, picking herbs. She plucked meadowsweet and thyme to scatter in the deer milk. Afterwards, she heated the milk and herbs in a pot over the fire, making a thick cheese called croudie. This was the old woman's life.

The girl went everywhere with the old woman, watching her at her work until, one day, she took over the old woman's work. Thus, the old woman's life became the girl's life.

When the croudie was ready, it was given to the old man, who sat day and night by the pool.

'What is that pool?' the girl asked the old woman one day.

'It is the Pool of Life,' the old woman answered.

Once he had the bucket, the old man would take a lump of croudie in his hands. Staring into the depths of the pool, he would fashion the croudie into shapes and figures.

'What are those shapes he makes?' asked the girl one evening.

'They are dreams,' said the old woman. 'We are the Makers of Dreams.'

Every evening, the old man took the bucket to the rocky buttress overlooking the western sea. As the sun scattered gold over the mountains, he held up his works in his hands, one by one.

In his right hand, he held up dreams of love and joy, hope, bravery and brotherhood. As he held up each dream, a bird would fly down and take it from his hand. Eagles, falcons and kestrels came, and even little wrens. They took the dreams and carried them out into the world, gifting them to sleepers the world over.

In his left hand, the old man held aloft dreams of hatred, envy, distrust and jealousy. These dreams were borne away and sown among sleepers by kites, crows and all the birds of the battlefield; a dark harvest they would wait to reap.

One morning, the old woman roused the girl from her sleeping place by the fire.

'It is time for you to leave,' said the old woman. 'A year and a night have passed. You have served us well, and your reward awaits you.'

The girl was sad to hear this, for she had grown to love her life there. She would miss spending nights by their fire, gazing into the shifting and shimmering waters of the Pool of Life. Yet she did miss her family, her friends and her home.

The old woman called the lead hind in and spoke to her

in a whisper. Once she had finished, the hind led the girl out of the cave.

The herd gathered and led the girl out of the glen, down a path she had never noticed before. Down they went, ever down. In the evening, they reached a cove at the foot of the mountains, facing west.

'Thank you,' said the girl. 'I'll miss you all.' She hugged each of the hinds and made to leave, but they crowded around her. They wouldn't let her leave. Every one of them was looking west.

She followed their gaze. Raising her hand to shield her eyes from the sun, she saw what they were looking at. Rowing towards her, in a little coracle, was a man.

The man beached his craft and climbed out. He was young, perhaps a little older than her, and wore a golden torque around his neck.

He was a prince.

The Prince walked over to her. The hinds parted and bowed to him as he bowed before her.

'My Lady, he said, 'I have crossed the ocean in search of you, and at last I have found you.

'I come from Tir Na Nog, the Land of the Ever Young, which lies further west than West. Every night, for a year and a night, I have dreamed of you. I have seen you milking hinds, gathering herbs and gazing into the Pool of Life.

'As I dreamed of you, I fell in love with you. I ask you now to come with me, over the sea to Tir Na Nog, and marry me.

Be my bride, rule over our people and teach us the meaning of dreams.'

The girl had fallen in love with the man before he even spoke. Though she longed to see her family and friends, her time by the pool had taught her wisdom. Her destiny lay over the waves.

Again, the girl said goodbye to the hinds. She turned, took the Prince's hand and waded into the water. They climbed into the coracle and crossed the sea to Tir Na Nog. She lives there now, and she will live there until the end of days.[1]

---

1. *This is a favourite among Scotland's storytellers, for obvious reasons. Besides its beauty, it has the feeling of a gateway into the ancient past. It was collected by Otta Swire and features in her 1952 collection,* Skye: The Island and Its Legends, *which went on to influence Neil Gaiman. The Cuillins are named after the Irish hero, Cuchulainn, who trained as a warrior on Skye with the witch queen, Scathach. The next book in this series will focus on Cuchulainn, while Scathach features in my forthcoming novel,* The Spey Queen.

    Tir Na Nog, the mythical island mentioned here, is commonly referred to in Irish legends but less so in Scotland. It is a place where everything is perfect, where no-one gets old or speaks ill of another. Tir Na Nog lies behind Valinor, the undying land which the elves sail to in The Lord Of The Rings. *Ossian, Finn MacCoull's son, spent many years here. You can find Ossian's story in* Finn & The Fianna, *my collection of Fianna tales.*

15

THE CATTLE OF PABBAY

A little island named Mingulay lies in the South of the Outer Hebrides. Just north of Mingulay is an even smaller island called Pabbay, and something very strange once happened there.

A couple once moved from Mingulay to Pabbay to take over a small farm, known in the highlands and islands as a croft. It was no great change; both islands consist of nothing more than cliffs and boggy moors, with one cove and a few acres of passable farmland in the east. At that time, the Hebridean people lived in close proximity to their animals. The blackhouses were built so that the house was split down the middle. One half was for the people, the other for the animals.

The couple arrived at the croft. They took a look around

and when they inspected the byre, they got a shock. There was already a cow there.

'I never paid for any cow,' the man said to his wife. 'Do you know anything about this?'

She didn't, and neither did any of their neighbours. There was nothing for it but to be grateful for their good fortune.

The couple got to work. They prepared the fields for planting, mended tools and decorated the house. Both of them worked hard and soon their croft was thriving. They were happy.

The cow gave them a calf that year, and another the next year. The herd grew steadily over the years, and always gave rich, frothy milk. The couple were very fond of their cows, particularly the old matriarch. She had an air of peace and even wisdom about her, and they often talked to her while working in the byre.

As the years went by, the old grandmother cow increasingly showed the signs of her age. She preferred to stay in the byre, moving ever more slowly and growing increasingly thin. One autumn, her milk dried up altogether.

A week or so later, the couple were sitting by their fire in the evening when the husband brought up the subject he dreaded.

'I've got something to say, and you won't want to hear it,' he said.

'I know what you're going to say,' said his wife. 'And you're right, I don't want to hear it.'

'We can't afford to feed a cow all winter, knowing she won't milk and won't calf.'

'But she's such a lovely creature. I'm awfully fond of her.'

'So am I; but what must be done, must be done. You needn't be involved, I'll take care of it.'

His wife was grateful for that. 'I'm going to bed,' she said, too upset to talk anymore.

With a heavy heart, her husband prepared his tools. He laid out and scrubbed clean a set of buckets for the flesh, fat and bones. He sharpened his knives, sharpened his cleaver and filled buckets with salted water for the meat. Finally, he joined his wife in bed.

The next morning, he awoke early. Without giving himself time to contemplate his day's work, he got out of bed, gathered his things and walked around the house to the byre door.

The door was wide open.

In he ran. The byre was empty. Not a single one of their cows was to be seen. On the ground outside was a mass of hoof prints.

He followed the hoof prints. They led him over the fields and down to the beach. At the water's edge, they disappeared.

He couldn't understand it. Had someone driven his herd into the sea? It made no sense. He rushed home and woke his wife, who could make no sense of it either. They decided to visit a neighbour and ask their opinion.

The closest croft belonged to an elderly man who'd lived there since the day he was born. He welcomed them in and they sat down to talk.

'Well,' he said after hearing their story, 'I think I understand what's happened here.

'If I remember rightly, you came by when you first took over the croft. You said there was already a cow in the byre and wondered whom it might belong to. Is that right?'

'It is,' said the wife.

'Were you fond of the cow?'

'We were,' said the wife. 'We were awfully fond of her. She was so peaceful, so clever. It was as if she understood what you said to her.'

The neighbour nodded, as if this all made sense. 'I didn't say so at the time,' he said, 'for it's sometimes better not to speak of such things; better just to let them be.

'That cow you found in your byre was a fairy cow. She came from the sea, to live with you and help you in your life here. You were good and kind to her, you treated her well, so she stayed and gave you a fine herd. But last night, when you talked about putting an end to her, she must have heard you through the wall. She didn't fancy having a knife put through her throat, so she's left. Into the sea she'll have gone, and her whole herd with her.'

The couple returned home. They prayed for the old cow

and her herd to come home, but they never did. Thankfully they had enough money put away to start a new herd; but they never stopped missing their fairy cow.[1]

---

1. *Thank you again to Ian Stephen for this story. It can be found in his magnificent collection of Hebridean stories,* Western Isles Folk Tales. *The sea is ever-present in stories from the Hebrides, which lie at the very edge of the Eurasian continent. Belief in fairy cattle was once widespread there. It was said that scattering soil from a churchyard along the shore would prevent them from returning to the sea, forcing them to remain on land.*

The name Pabbay comes from 'Papey', which is Norse for 'Island of the Papar (Monks)'. The island was a hermitage for Celtic christian monks. It was abandoned after most of the male inhabitants of the island were killed during a storm in 1897.

16

THE KING & THE COCKEREL

Along time ago, when Scotland had its own king, the King lived in Edinburgh Castle. He was a wealthy man. The King had mountains of jewels, heaps of gold and silver, fine clothes to wear and the best food to eat every day. Despite all that, he was an unhappy man, for however much he had, he always wanted more.

The King's favourite pastime was to climb into his carriage and head out into the city to collect taxes. He especially liked collecting taxes from poor people.

One autumn afternoon, he set out in his carriage. His driver cracked the whip, the gates of the castle opened and the horses sped down the cobbled streets.

On the poorest street in the city lived the poorest old woman in Scotland. Her house was nothing more than some old planks of wood nailed together, and she had nothing but a sack with holes in it to wear. For all that, she was a much happier person than the King, for she had something he didn't have. She had friends. Her friends were her three hens and her cockerel.

Every day, the hens and the cockerel would wander around her garden, looking for worms to eat. The hens laid eggs which she ate for every meal. On that particular afternoon, the hens and the cockerel were wandering through the garden, looking for juicy worms to eat, when the cockerel crowed in excitement.

He had found something. From among the grass he plucked a golden penny. He held it up towards the sun, it shone in the sunlight and, in that moment, the King drove up outside the house in his carriage.

'Stop!' he roared to his driver.

The driver stopped and the King climbed out of the carriage. He walked over to the old woman's gate, kicked it down and marched over to the cockerel. The King snatched the penny from the cockerel's mouth.

'I'll take that,' he said with a sneer. 'Taxes.'

The King got back into his carriage. The driver cracked the whip again and off they went, back to Edinburgh Castle. That might have been the end of that; but this was no ordinary cockerel.

The cockerel flapped his wings. He flew into the air, higher and higher, until he spotted the carriage winding its way through the streets. He followed it, all the way up the

Royal Mile, until the carriage came to a halt in the castle courtyard.

The King climbed out and brushed off his robe. He was looking forward to his dinner, and was about to make his way over to the royal dining room when the cockerel landed in front of him. It crowed at him and shouted, 'Give me back my penny! Give me back my penny!'

The King was both flustered and furious. 'Guards! Guards!' he called.

A group of guards came running.

'Take this accursed cockerel,' said the King, 'and throw him into the royal well.'

The guards seized the cockerel by his scrawny neck, marched him over to the well and threw him in.

The cockerel sank to the bottom of the well. What could he do?

He opened his beak and drank up all the water in the well. He drank and drank until there was none left, and then he beat his wings. It was hard, since he was full of so much water, but he managed to take off and fly out of the well. Over the courtyard he flew.

Meanwhile, the King was sitting down to eat in the royal dining room. An enormous fire roared at the end of the room and before him on the table was a spread of fruits and vegetables, cheeses and meats, whiskies and wines. He was just spreading his napkin on his lap when the cockerel landed on the windowsill and shouted, 'Give me back my penny! Give me back my penny!'

The King spluttered and called for his guards. They came running.

'Take this accursed cockerel,' he said, 'and throw him into the royal fire!'

The guards seized the cockerel by his scrawny neck. They marched him over to the fire, which was so big that entire trees were burning on it, and threw him in.

The cockerel shot through the air, spinning around as he flew towards the flames. The moment he touched them, he would be burnt to a crisp.

What could he do?

He opened his mouth. As he flew towards the fire, he let out a great jet of water; all the water that had filled the royal well. It soaked the fire, dowsing the flames. When he landed, he landed on a cold, wet soup of logs and ashes.

Unfortunately, the King had seen it all.

'Guards! Guards!' he cried.

The guards were ready and waiting.

'Take this accursed cockerel,' said the King, 'and throw him into the royal beehive.'

The guards seized the cockerel by his scrawny neck. They led him out of the castle and into the royal gardens. They opened the door of the beehive, threw the cockerel in and slammed the door shut behind him.

Now the cockerel was in real trouble. He was surrounded

by swarming, buzzing bees and he was an intruder in their hive.

What could he do?

He ate the bees, of course. One by one, he snapped them up until his stomach was full of them; then he kicked down the door of the beehive and set off to confront the King, one last time.

The King was in his bedroom, getting ready for bed. He had put on his pyjamas and was sitting at his dressing table, combing his hair, when the cockerel landed on his windowsill.

Again, and even louder than before, the cockerel shouted, 'Give me back my penny! Give me back my penny!'

The King leapt from his seat. Seeing the cockerel, he was about to call for the guards; but he decided it against it. The guards were useless. It was time to deal with the cockerel himself.

The King sauntered casually over to the cockerel.

He grabbed him by his scrawny neck. With a manic cackle, he stuffed the cockerel down the back of his pyjama bottoms.

Roaring with laughter, the King sat down on the edge of his bed, squashing the cockerel between the bed and his buttocks.

Can you guess what happened?

Of course you can. The cockerel opened his mouth and

out shot the entire swarm of enraged bees. Every single one of them stung the King on his bottom.

The King leapt into the air, roaring with pain. He ran around and around his bedchamber, swatting at his bottom as the cockerel squirmed out and flew around the room.

The guards burst into the chamber. The King cried out, 'Give him back his penny! Give him back his penny!'

One of the guards spotted the penny on the King's nightstand. He grabbed it and threw it towards the cockerel. The cockerel caught it in his mouth and flew out of the window.

Over the sleeping city he flew. The next morning, when the poor old woman opened her front door, the cockerel was waiting for her with the golden penny in his mouth.

The old woman was overjoyed. She bought some wood and nails with which to build a new house, and treated herself to a new sack to wear.[1]

---

1. *I heard this story from Ron Fairweather, who performs as part of the riotous duo Macastory. It has a counterpart in the American story of* The Rooster and The Pearl.

   There are many Russian stories in which cockerels are associated with kings, and lay golden eggs; probably because of their association with the sun. It is interesting to note the cockerel's association with gold and the sun, which often symbolise the divine or archetypal king, and contrast it with the petty, childish king we meet in the story. The cockerel is directly associated with air, fire, water and earth, and is in union with the feminine, while the King is defined by his own sense of incompleteness. It's fascinating to see how much can lie behind a seemingly simple story.

17

ASIPATTLE AND THE STOOR WORM

The North coast of Scotland is both bleak and beautiful. Its inhabitants are no strangers to storms, nor to cold, hunger or bruising rain. When you stand on the cliffs of Cape Wrath, there is nothing but seawater between you and the Arctic ice.

It is fitting that one of Scotland's most magnificent tales comes from the far North.

The story begins in a tiny village, clinging to the cliffs above the wild ocean. The people there were fishers and farmers, who tied their children to posts to stop the wind from carrying them over the cliffs. They had as many children as they could, for most would not live beyond their first few years. Those that grew into fishers and farmers would often go to their graves early, ground down by illness or stolen by the sea. Yet the people there prevailed; up until the night the stoor worm struck.

From an abyss far beyond the edge of any map, the maester stoor worm came to Caithness. Waves pounded the shore as the titanic serpent arose out of the ocean, gulls shrieking as they fled its great maw.

Looking down on the dark coast, the stoor worm spied the village and smelt the men and women who lived there. Though it subsisted on whales, the stoor worm was fond of human flesh. It roared a roar that rattled the entire world; then it began to feed.

It smashed stone houses to dust with its snout. Villagers fleeing their homes were snapped up and devoured. The stoor worm ate every single villager before retreating to the deep sea.

It struck again the next night, and the night after that. Village after village was destroyed. Refugees began to desert the coast, heading inland to seek the protection of their king.

The King of Caithness resided in a modest timber castle. He was not a bad man, but not an especially good or intelligent one either.

'Be calm,' he told his subjects. 'I shall send fighting men to deal with this beast, and they will bring me its head soon enough.'

A company of fighting men was sent out to patrol the coast. Their captain instructed the villagers to post lookouts each day, and to light beacon fires when the shadow of the stoor worm darkened the sea. This they did, and soon the fighting men came face to face with the stoor worm.

It ate them.

The King was at a loss. Hungry villagers were crowding his court and eating their way through his grain stores. What was he do?

One evening, as the King sat picking at his dinner plate, a serving man summoned up the courage to address him. He told the King that he knew of a sorcerer, who lived deep within the mountains and marshes of Assynt. The serving man was from Assynt himself, and many people from his village had procured the sorcerer's cures, curses, charms and ointments. Perhaps the sorcerer could help with this matter?

The King had no better ideas. He left his castle the next day, the serving man guiding his small retinue through the glens and over the moors to Assynt.

There, beneath a mountain that resembled a sleeping dragon, they came to the sorcerer's hut.

In went the King. The sorcerer had been expecting him and invited him to sit down by the fire. Herbs, woven charms and the dried corpses of rodents hung from the rafters.

'Can you help me?' asked the King, after explaining his predicament.

'I know of the stoor worm,' said the sorcerer, 'and I have already consulted the bones. They say that the only way to deal with the worm is to feed it seven maidens, every Sunday. The bones gave me the names of the first seven. Offer them to the stoor worm tomorrow evening and your subjects will be safe.'

The King was shocked. He didn't want to feed the young women of his kingdom to a sea monster; but it seemed he had no choice.

The sorcerer accompanied the King and his men to the castle, and the next day, seven maidens were rounded up and tied to posts on a beach.

The stoor worm came. It ate them up and it left. It wasn't seen again until it returned a week later for the next seven maidens.

Peace returned to the kingdom, though it was a desolate peace. Villagers went home to their villages; fishermen went out fishing again. It was a relief to go to sleep without expecting to be devoured in the night. Yet, everyone feared that their own daughter or granddaughter would be next in line for the stoor worm's stomach.

Every Monday, the sorcerer read the bones and announced the names of the next seven sacrifices.

One day, the seventh name he spoke was 'Gem De Lovely'.

Princess Gem De Lovely.

'What? No! Give me another name!' said the King.

'The bones have spoken,' said the sorcerer.

'Summon my heralds,' said the King.

The heralds were brought before the King. Soon they were rushing out of the gates to recite the King's proclamation throughout the land.

'The King seeks a warrior,' announced a herald in every marketplace, 'strong enough to slay the stoor worm. That warrior shall marry the Princess, and shall inherit the King's sword and his kingdom; but only if the stoor worm is destroyed before the next sacrifice.'

Word reached the ears of every warrior in the kingdom. Not one of them came forward.

In one particular village, on one particular farm, a husband and wife lived with their seven sons. Six of those sons were strong, strapping lads, whose only desire in life was to work harder than they had done on the previous day. Their mother and father couldn't have been more proud of them.

The seventh son was different. He didn't dream of working harder, for he didn't work at all. Instead, he spent his days and nights lying in front of the fire, a light dusting of ash upon him. With his eyes half-closed, he flew through the sky on the back of a winged bear; he swam with dolphin-men, slaughtered monsters and rescued an endless stream of princesses.

His mother, father and brothers despised him. They kicked him every time they passed him. His name was Asipattle, which means 'Cinder-Biter'.

Six days after the King made his proclamation, on the evening before Princess Gem De Lovely was due to be sacrificed, the news reached Asipattle's farm. His eldest brother came in from the market, sat down at the table and repeated the words of the proclamation. The word around the market was that not a single warrior had taken up the challenge.

At that moment, Asipattle did something unexpected.

He stood up, shook the ashes from his clothes and addressed his family.

'I shall slay the stoor worm!' he said. 'I shall marry Princess Gem De Lovely and inherit the kingdom!'

His family laughed so much that several of them were sick.

Asipattle paid them no mind. He lay back down beside the fire. When it was dark outside, and his family were asleep, he rose up again.

He lined his stomach with leftovers and went out to the stables. There he saddled his father's finest horse, a white mare named Teetgong, which means 'Gust of Wind'. He opened her stable door, climbed onto her back and rode out into the night.

By moonlight, he galloped down the coast. Teetgong's name proved to be apt, for she went as fast as the wind. Asipattle soon arrived at the beach where the sacrifices were made each week. Seven posts stood on the sands.

Asipattle spied a hut at the far end of the beach. An upturned boat sat on the sands nearby.

He led the horse to the hut, dismounted and crept into the hut. By the soft light of fire-embers, he saw an old woman sleeping. Very quietly, Asipattle took her pot and filled it with peats from the fire. He silently promised the old woman that he would return her pot, before slipping away.

Outside, Asipattle righted the fishing boat, dragged it to the water and climbed in. The pot of peats between his feet, he rowed out onto the silvery ocean.

Out at sea, Asipattle pulled in his oars and waited.

Hours passed.

Just as Asipattle was beginning to doubt his luck, the sea stirred before him. From out of the water rose the head of the stoor worm, opening its mouth to take a breath.

Asipattle rowed furiously for the stoor worm's open jaws. Just before they snapped shut, he leapt from his boat onto the tip of its tongue. The stoor worm's mouth closed and it dived for the depths again; only now, it was carrying Asipattle in its mouth.

Down the stoor worm's squishy tongue he ran. Asipattle's stomach churned at the awful smells as he entered its throat and raced down its great length, a cathedral of bones towering over him, the old woman's pot clutched in his hand.

After running for miles, far beneath the waves, Asipattle reached the stoor worm's stomach.

Clouds of stinking gas filled the air. Asipattle covered his mouth, his skin burning as he stumbled through the vapours, keeping close to the stomach wall, until he found what he was looking for.

The entrance to the stoor worm's liver.

Asipattle wasted no time. He took the lid off the pot, pulled open the narrow opening leading to the liver and emptied into it the contents of the pot.

Asipattle turned and ran.

As he ran, he felt the stoor worm begin to tremble. It shook, writhed and roared as it surged towards the surface.

The worm erupted from the sea. Its roar launched Asipattle into the sky. He flew over the churning sea and landed on the beach, right in front of the King and Princess Gem De Lovely, who had ridden there for the sacrifice.

They barely noticed him, for they were staring out to sea. He turned and saw that they had good reason to stare.

The stoor worm was on fire. It thrashed about, churning

the ocean to milk in its agony. So great was its roar that its teeth came loose, shot out of its mouth and landed in the sea.

The stoor worm's molars are still there, scattered in the sea north of Scotland. They are the islands of Orkney and Shetland. Its fangs are there too, further north; they are called Faroe. At one point, the stoor worm reared up, wrapped its tongue around the horn of the moon (for the moon had a horn, back then) and pulled it off. The horn crashed down on Scandinavia, creating the Baltic Sea. As for the stoor worm's body, it is still out there, churning and smoking and burning. You probably know it as Iceland.

Back on the beach, the growing crowd of onlookers watched the stoor worm burn for a while, then turned to Asipattle. He seemed like someone with a story to tell.

Asipattle obliged them, telling his tale with eloquence and wit as the stoor worm burned behind him. His story was hard to deny, given the entrance he had made. Asipattle married Princess Gem De Lovely. He claimed the King's sword, Sikkersnapper, and in time became King.

King Asipattle and Queen Gem De Lovely ruled over Caithness until they were old and grey. Their children were always encouraged to lie by the fire, dreaming of impossible things.[1]

---

1. *This is a very special story from me. I first heard it from Erin Farley, and many years later it became the basis of my novel,* The Shattering Sea. *There is a raw, elemental power to the north coast of Scotland which, to me, this*

story expresses. Standing on those cliffs, it is easy to believe that the deep sea contains giants unknown to us.

I changed a few elements of this story. In the version commonly heard, Asipattle borrows a goose thrapple from his father, which he blows through to make Teetgong go faster. I omitted it as it doesn't fit the tone of my telling. I would encourage you to read Tom Muir's Orkney Folk Tales *if you wish to get to know this story better.*

18

THE WELL OF YOUTH

The highlands of Scotland are nowadays mostly owned by bankers and businessmen, who visit their estates to strut around in tweed and shoot little birds. In days gone by, those same estates were owned by lairds, who collected rent from the people living on their land.

Their tenants were crofters, who fished and farmed and worked the land to raise their rent money. Rather than collecting the rent himself, the laird would send round his secretary, who was known as the factor.

There were kind factors and cruel factors. On one particular estate, lying deep among the Affric hills, the Laird's factor was a warm and generous man. Though he worked for the Laird, he counted the crofters as his friends. He liked to stop in and chat at every house, checking that all was well, and if anyone was late with the rent, he always allowed them time to find the money.

In one of the houses lived an old couple named Angus and Bessie. Angus and Bessie had reached an age where their work grew more difficult each day, and every year their harvest was smaller. The day eventually came when they had no money with which to pay their rent.

Unfortunately for them, the Laird's factor had died earlier that month. The Laird had a new factor, and he was said to be a different sort of man.

A knock came at the door on rent day. Angus opened it, and there stood the new factor.

'Angus and Bessie,' he said, 'I am the Laird's new factor. Your rent is due.'

'Oh, good morning,' said Angus. It's lovely to meet you–'

'Don't waste my time,' said the factor. 'Your rent is due and I am here to collect it, not to stand around gossiping.'

'Ah, yes, well, I'm afraid we don't have it just yet. If you could come back in a couple of weeks–'

'I will come back, Angus, but it won't be in two weeks. I shall return tomorrow, and if you don't have your rent money ready, I will turn you out of this house.'

The factor turned around and marched away down the road.

Angus and Bessie were beside themselves. They sat down at the table and tried to come up with a plan. They discussed borrowing from this person or that person, but it was no good; whatever they borrowed, they would be unable to pay back.

Angus chewed his lip. 'I think I might have an idea, Bessie,' he said.

'What is it?'

'Did you ever hear folk talking of the Well of Youth?'

'The Well of Youth?' said Bessie.

'Aye, the Well of Youth,' said Angus.

'When I was young,' he went on, 'I heard a man say that there's a well in the hills behind our house, a spring. Whoever drinks from it, he said, will be given the gift of youth. If we drank its water and were young again, we could work hard to pay back any money we borrowed.'

Bessie thought this was all very odd, but she had no better idea to offer. The next morning, they donned their coats and set off into the hills.

It was wearying to climb the steep paths at their age, especially since they didn't know exactly where they were going. Fortunately, it was a fine day, or they might never have made it home again. They reached the high ridges and wandered here and there until Bessie cried out with excitement.

'Look, Angus! It's a spring!'

Angus joined her and peered at the spring she'd found.

'Do you think this might be it?' he said.

'Only one way to find out.'

Angus bent down and scooped up some water in his hands. He put them to his lips and took a tiny sip.

He looked at Bessie. 'Well? Did it work?'

Bessie didn't answer. She was looking at him in a way she hadn't looked at him for a long time.

'Oh, Angus,' she said. 'My gorgeous husband.'

She stepped closer to him. In her eyes, Angus saw himself reflected. He was no longer an old, bent-backed, grey-haired man; he was tall and broad, muscular and bright-eyed, just as he had once been.

'My turn,' said Bessie. She knelt over the spring, took a drink and looked at Angus.

'Well?' she said.

Angus didn't say anything. He couldn't say anything; he could only stare at the red-haired and red-lipped beauty standing before him.

He kissed her. She kissed him back, and many hours passed before they headed home.

The factor hammered on their door the following morning.

'Angus! Bessie! Open this door!'

The door opened.

'You'd better have your... oh, I beg your pardon,' said the factor to the young couple standing before him. 'I'm looking for Angus and Bessie.'

'That's us,' said Bessie.

'Nonsense!' snorted the factor. 'You are a fine-looking young pair; Angus and Bessie are doddering old fools.'

Angus gave him a thin smile. 'Nevertheless, we are Angus and Bessie.' He told the factor the whole story.

He finished his story and handed over the rent money, which he'd borrowed from a neighbour. 'There you go,' said Angus. 'Lovely to see you.'

'What? Oh, yes... and to see you...' the factor turned and ran away.

'Where do you think he's going?' asked Angus.

'I have an idea,' said Bessie.

A few days later, a neighbour stopped by for a gossip. She mentioned that the factor had not been by to collect the rent, from her nor from anyone else.

'I think,' said Bessie to Angus, after their neighbour had left, 'that we'd better take a walk again.'

They left the house and climbed up into the hills. Retracing their steps, they arrived at the Well of Youth.

Lying among the heather was a baby.

Angus and Bessie took the baby home. They raised him as if he were their own, and under their influence he grew to be a fine lad; kind, courteous and hard-working.

When Angus and Bessie died, the lad took over the

running of their croft. He married and had children, and no-one around there ever had a bad word to say about him. A good many folk did remark, though, on his uncanny resemblance to the old factor.[1]

---

1. *This is a lovely little story which I heard from David Campbell, the Grand High Elf of Scottish storytellers and my dear friend and mentor. It relates to the Cauldron of Rebirth, a mythical artefact found in the Irish story of* The Battle of Moytura *and the Welsh story of* Bran the Blessed. *There are tales, too, of the Cailleach having her youth restored when she drinks from the waters of Ben Cruachan.*

   You can listen to Michael Harvey tell the story of Bran the Blessed *as* Branwen *on* House of Legends Podcast *and on his own podcast,* Mabinogi Mondays.

   The Cauldron of Rebirth relates to the Holy Grail, and also to the Cup of Healing, which features in The Daughter Of King Under Wave, *a classic Fianna legend, and in* The Snake Shirt.

19

THE MERMAID BRIDE

On the Isle of Sanday in Orkney, there once lived a man named Johnny Croy. Johnny lived on a farm in Volyar with his mother, and he was unmarried. He wasn't likely to remain that way for long. He was tall and handsome, with beautiful blue eyes and an easy laugh, and there was hardly a woman on the island who didn't blush when she saw him.

One summer's day, Johnny left the farm to visit the beach in search of driftwood. There are few trees in Orkney, so wood is a precious substance.

Johnny reached the beach and strolled along the white sand. It was a perfect day. The sky was as blue as the sea, the sea was as blue as the sky and both were as blue as Johnny's bright eyes. He saw no driftwood, so on he went, until he came to a headland and stopped to listen.

On the other side of the dunes, he could hear someone singing.

That wasn't so unusual; but he'd never heard singing like this before. This song rose and fell with the grace of starlings in flight. It made him want to lie down and fall asleep, to leap up and dance, to laugh and to cry all at once.

He climbed the dunes. On the next stretch of sand, a woman sat on a rock, facing out to sea. She was combing her long, golden hair which tumbled like a waterfall down her back. Tied around her waist was a fish-tail, which she wore like a skirt.

She was, of course, a mermaid. Orkney's mermaids are said to have human legs, with a fish-tail they can tie around their waists and remove, should they wish to.

Johnny was entranced. He approached the mermaid and stood directly in front of her, as ecstatic as a leaping dolphin in the ocean of her song.

The mermaid ceased singing.

She opened her eyes.

Johnny was standing right in front of her. She gave a yelp of fright, and before she could dash away, Johnny bent down and kissed her.

He drew back. She drew back. He looked as surprised as she did.

The mermaid recovered herself. She smiled at Johnny and took her fish-tail in her hand.

Faster than a striking snake, she swung her tail and

slapped Johnny's face, knocking him to the ground. By the time he got to his feet, she was already in the water. She dived and disappeared from sight.

Johnny ran to the shore. There was no sign of her; but lying on the sand at his feet was her comb.

Johnny picked up the comb. It was made of polished bone and engraved with swirling patterns. He looked out to sea.

The mermaid was bobbing up and down on the water.

'Give me my comb,' she called to him.

'I'll give it to you if you marry me,' he said.

'Just give it to me, please.'

'Marry me and I'll give you my heart.'

'I can't marry you,' she said. 'I'm a mermaid, I belong in the sea. Toss me my comb, please.'

'But you have legs, you can walk, you'd be fine living on the land. I'd look after you and treat you well and...'

Voices reached him on the wind. He looked behind him and when he looked out to sea again, the mermaid was gone.

Johnny walked home. Or rather, he floated home. He sat at the table, his mother put a bowl of stew in front of him and he didn't even notice it was there.

Johnny's mother sat down opposite him. She took note of his faraway look and his dreamy smile.

'You've met a lass, haven't you, Johnny?' she said.

'Aye,' said Johnny.

His mother sighed. She didn't believe that any woman in the world could be good enough for her son.

'Alright, then,' she said. 'Who is she? Is it that Mary?'

'No,' said Johnny.

'Is it the Muir girl?'

No,' said Johnny.

'The Flett girl?'

'No.'

His mother frowned. 'She's not from Shapinsay, is she?'

'No, Mum, she's not from Shapinsay. She's... she's a mermaid.'

Silence shrouded the room.

'A mermaid, Johnny?' said his mother at last.

'Aye.'

Johnny's mother sighed again. She snapped her fingers in front of her son's eyes.

'Now you just listen to me, Johnny Croy,' she said. 'And listen well. You're a Christian boy. This is a Christian household, and we'll have no dealings with mermaids here. Finfolk, mermaids, trowies, silkies; they're all the Devil's creatures. Do you understand me?'

Johnny looked down at his plate. 'Yes, Mother, I understand.'

'I hope so,' said his mother.

Johnny went to sleep that night thinking of her. He

woke up thinking of her, and in every quiet moment he took out her comb and stroked it, tracing its patterns with his fingers.

Time passed. At first, Johnny was ablaze with joy. He had met the woman he was born to love; they would be together soon and never part. Every day he roved the beaches, waiting for her to show herself. Surely, she would come to him. It was only a matter of time.

She didn't come to him. He saw seals, ducks and porpoises, but no golden-haired mermaid. His joy soured; despair took him. Johnny pined for the mermaid day and night, talons of despair steadily sinking into his heart.

Finally, after yet another sleepless night, Johnny slipped out of bed in the half-light before dawn and crossed the island.

He was going to see the spey-wife.

A spey-wife is the Orcadian name for a witch. There was one spey on Sanday, a one-eyed old woman who served the old gods. None of the God-fearing islanders would admit to procuring her charms and spells, but there were plenty who did so in secret.

The spey-wife wasn't surprised to hear a rap on her door in the early hours of morning. She ushered Johnny in and sat him down by her fire.

'What's your trouble?' she asked him.

'It's a girl,' said Johnny.

'What a surprise,' said the spey-wife with a smile.

Johnny told her his story. She listened carefully, without interrupting.

'Well then,' she said when he finished. 'I've something to say to you, Johnny, and it's not what you want to hear.

'You need to forget this woman. I know how you feel, and how you're suffering. But you're not the first Orcadian to fall for a mermaid, nor will you be the last. This has happened many times, Johnny. It's never ended well.

'That said, I know a few words from me won't stop you loving her. The web weaves as the web weaves. So, I'll tell you this. You have her comb?'

'Aye.'

'Keep it. A mermaid can only be without her comb for so long. If you keep it close, sooner or later she'll come to you.'

Johnny was so happy that he almost kissed the spey-wife. He gave her a bag of mussels and dashed home, a mad grin splitting his face.

A few nights later, Johnny awoke in the middle of the night from a dream of the mermaid's song. Lying awake, he could still hear her song.

Johnny opened his eyes. He sat up.

Sitting on the end of his bed, illuminated by moonlight streaming in through the window, was the mermaid.

She ceased singing.

'I knew you'd come for me,' said Johnny.

'I came for my comb,' she said.

'Marry me,' said Johnny.

'I told you, Johnny Croy,' she said. 'I belong in the sea. I can't marry you.'

'You can take off your fish-tail,' said Johnny. 'You could live here on the farm with me. I'll inherit the farm one day, and we'll have children of our own. We'll take them for walks on the beach and play with them by the fire in the evening. I love you, and I promise we'll have a good life together.'

'We could do that,' she said. 'Or we could live beneath the sea. We could live in a city of coral and crystal, far below the waves. Every day we could ride seals on the hunt, and every night we could dance amid a shimmering, shifting web of whale-song.'

'No, no,' said Johnny. 'I can't leave the farm. There's always been a Croy on this farm, and I couldn't be the last, not for anything.'

The mermaid thought for a while.

'Well, how about this then,' she said. 'I'll marry you. You shouldn't have kept my comb from me, but you're a good man. I see it in those bonny blue eyes of yours. I'll marry you, and live with you on the land for seven years. After that, you, me and any bairns we might have will live under the sea for seven years. If you still want to return to the land after seven years beneath the sea, we'll do so, for the rest of our lives. What do you say?'

'I say yes,' said Johnny. They kissed in the moonlight, and he gave her back her comb.

The news went out; Johnny Croy was to marry. It raced around the island and it was all anyone talked about, yet no-one knew who'd won Johnny's heart.

'Is it that Mary?' they asked.

'It's not Kate Muir?'

'Maybe it's Lizzy Flett?'

'She's not from Shapinsay, is she?'

The day of the wedding came. The islanders packed themselves into the church, waiting to get a glimpse of the girl who'd netted Johnny Croy.

Johnny waited at the altar.

The fiddlers took up the wedding music.

In through the doors walked Johnny's bride.

The congregation turned and gasped. It almost hurt their eyes to look at her, so beautiful was she in her white dress and pearls, with a rainbow of flowers adorning her golden hair.

She joined Johnny at the altar. The two smiled at one another as the minister opened his bible and began to read.

Something curious happened then. Johnny's bride began to fidget. She chewed her lips so hard that they bled. People noticed her pinching her arms and bringing her shoulder to her ear, as if to block out the minister's voice. The truth was that she couldn't stand the words of the bible, which are poisonous to creatures of magic.

She got through it. Johnny put his lips to hers, and they were married. There was a wedding party back at the farm, which Johnny's mother excused herself from, claiming she was feeling unwell. The happy couple and their guests danced and drank and had a wonderful time.

In the days and weeks after the wedding, it seemed as if half of Orkney found their way to Johnny's door. They each claimed to be passing by, or that they needed to borrow a hammer or a spade, but, really, they just wanted to learn more about Johnny's bride.

Everyone who visited found her a delight. Johnny's bride sang heart-rending songs, knew a sackful of riddles and brewed the best ale in Orkney. She was always willing to share her wonderful stories and songs, to offer another cog of ale or to lend a hand when needed. Though many a girl was jealous of her, and though many a man was jealous of Johnny, no-one could find a bad word to say about her.

In time, she grew pregnant. Everyone celebrated the news; but for one person.

Johnny's mother.

Her boy had never gone against her wishes until he met the sea creature. The fish-tailed witch had put a spell on Johnny, she was sure of it. Yet there was no telling Johnny; he never listened to anything she said any more.

Seeing the sea witch take over her house was more than Johnny's mother could bear. She gave up working. All day, she sat in her chair in the corner, making every scathing remark she could think to make. Johnny and his wife sickened of her, and eventually they just ignored her. When her first grandson was born, she called him devil-spawn and refused to touch him.

Seven years passed. Johnny and the mermaid were happily married, with seven healthy children to their name.

The time came for them to leave Sanday.

They made their plans in secret. Johnny was afraid to tell his mother; he put it off until the last moment, against his wife's wishes. But his mother eavesdropped and learnt what was happening.

One Sunday, she stayed on after church to talk with the minster. She told him the whole story.

'The Devil is in your house, sure enough, Mrs Croy,' he said. 'I only wish you had told me sooner.'

'Can anything be done?'

'Oh yes,' said the minister. 'There is something.'

The day of the move came. A boat rose out of the sea near their home. It was manned by finmen, who rowed it into shore.

They came to the house. Johnny and the finmen packed up everything they would be taking and brought it all down to the boat, while Johnny's wife kept the children from running beneath their feet.

'We're going on an adventure!' she told the children, who cheered and danced when they heard this.

Soon, they were ready to leave. Johnny had arranged with friends that they would take over the farm and look after his mother; he told them he would be staying with his wife's family for a while.

'I'll go and get the baby,' said Johnny's wife. They had gathered at the shore with the finmen; all the children save the youngest were in the boat.

She walked to the house. Inside, she took a last look around before entering the little back room where the baby slept in his cot.

It was dark and quiet in the room. The baby was sleeping. Johnny's wife leaned over the cot and reached down. She carefully took hold of her baby... and screamed.

Her hands leapt back as if burned. Pain shot up her arms and she looked in disbelief as the skin on her hands cracked and peeled.

Again, she tried to pick up her child. Again, she screamed as the same thing happened.

A terrible suspicion dawned on her.

She reached down again. This time, she didn't touch her baby's skin. Instead, she pulled back the covers and carefully lifted the little jumper he wore.

'No,' she said. 'No...'

Gouged into his back was a bloody cross.

Laughter sounded behind her.

Sitting among the shadows in the corner of the room was Johnny's mother.

'You thought you'd won, didn't you, Devil-woman,' she said. 'You may have stolen my boy from me. You might take the rest of my grandchildren from me. But not this one. This lad will grow up to be a Christian. He'll farm this land until he dies, just as his father should have done, and his children will do.'

There was nothing Johnny's wife could say or do. She left the room and left her baby.

'Where's–' began Johnny when she arrived at the boat.

'Go,' she said, shaking her head, not looking at anyone. 'Just go.'

Johnny saw the look in her eyes. He nodded to the finmen. They rowed the boat out to sea, and it disappeared beneath the waves.

Johnny and his family never returned to Sanday. Nothing more is known of them, so they must have chosen to live out their lives on the seabed.

As for their baby, the boy grew up and took over the farm. His name was Corsa Croy, meaning Croy of the Cross. Despite his grandmother's wishes, he became not a farmer but a warrior, fighting in far-of lands with strange-sounding names.

Corsa eventually married a Jarl's daughter and settled with her in Caithness. The farm at Volyar was never again farmed by a Croy.[1]

1. *I have a bit of a thing for Orkney (as you may have noticed), hence the plethora of Orcadian tales here; yet they really are fantastic. I love this story for its depiction of the coexistence of paganism with Christianity. I first encountered it in Tom Muir's* Orkney Folk Tales. *You can hear me telling this story on House of Legends Podcast.*

Combs are a common symbol in folklore, often associated with sea creatures and with magic. Paintings of combs have been found from as early as 6000 BC, and combs and mirrors were inscribed on Pictish stones.

20

THE SEAL HUNTER

On the Caithness coast, there once lived a man called Duncan MacKinnon. Duncan was a seal hunter. He lived in a little house at the edge of the beach, within a cove surrounded by high cliffs. Every day, he went out hunting seals. He pounced on them as they lay on the sand and stuck his great knife into them. Every evening, he dressed and treated the skins to prepare them for sale at the market.

Though Duncan loved the hunt, he had a code of honour. He would never harm a seal pup.

Duncan was skilled at every part of his work, so his skins always fetched a good price at the market, and Duncan was a fairly well-off man. He never got round to spending his money, though; he was only interested in hunting seals.

One stormy evening, Duncan sat by his fire with a dram

of whisky in hand, muttering and cursing to himself. He was in a foul mood, for that morning he'd lost his hunting knife. A seal had got away from him with his knife sheathed in its back. He could buy another one, of course, but he loved that knife. Outside, the weather was as black as his mood. Storm-winds rattled the window panes, hurling sheets of rain at the house as if trying to bring it down.

Duncan's bleak musings were interrupted by a knock at the door.

'Who could that be?' said Duncan to himself. He didn't get many visitors. None, in fact. He decided it must be someone looking to buy a skin. But who would come on a night like this?

He went to the door and opened it. Standing outside was a man. This man was tall, over six feet tall, with glittering brown eyes, deathly white skin and long, thick brown hair. He stared intently at Duncan.

'Good evening,' said Duncan, 'though it isn't a good evening. Can I help you?'

'You're Duncan MacKinnon?' said the man.

'Aye,' said Duncan.

'You're Duncan MacKinnon, the seal hunter?'

'Aye. Do you need a skin?'

'Yes,' said the man. 'Or rather, my friend does. I have a friend waiting nearby.'

'Well, I can sell your friend a skin,' said Duncan.

'He doesn't just want to buy one skin, Duncan. He wants to buy all your skins.'

'All my skins?' said Duncan. That was a lot of skins; a lot of money! But why come tonight? The whole business was very unusual. Yet Duncan was fond of making money, so he put the thought out of his mind.

'Well, bring your friend here, then,' said Duncan.

'No,' said the stranger. 'My friend won't come in here. He's waiting for us up on the cliff. Will you come?'

This was a queer business indeed; but there was money to be made, and Duncan needed a new hunting knife. He put on his coat and boots and headed out into the storm.

The stranger led him to the edge of the cove and up the path to the clifftops. As they walked, Duncan was already counting his earnings in his mind. Yet when they reached the clifftop, Duncan peered into the darkness and saw no-one.

'Where's your friend?' shouted Duncan over the howling wind.

'I don't know,' said the stranger. 'He should be here.'

The stranger walked over to the edge of the cliff. He looked down.

'Duncan!' said the stranger. 'I think he might have fallen over the cliff. Come and look!'

Duncan hurried over to where the stranger stood. He peered over the cliff.

The stranger put his arm around Duncan's back and swept him off the cliff.

Duncan tumbled through the air with the stranger's arms wrapped around him. They hit the water. Duncan writhed madly as he tried to escape, but the stranger was too strong. Black spots danced before his eyes, the world became faint and distant...

The stranger pulled him out of the water.

Duncan fell to his knees, vomiting seawater, gasping and coughing until he finally recovered his breath.

He looked around him.

They were in total darkness. Beneath his feet and hands was hard rock. He could hear nothing at all, save for the dripping of water on rock.

He was in a cave. A cave beneath the cliff.

Before he could speak, Duncan was hauled to his feet and dragged through the cave. He shivered and his teeth chattered as he walked.

Duncan saw light up ahead. They turned a corner and entered a grand cavern. It was ten times as large as his own house, its roof far above his head. Fires were scattered around the cave, giving off amber light that danced upon the cave-walls. Around the fires sat groups of pale-skinned and brown-haired men, women and children, none of them wearing clothes. They stared silently at Duncan, their eyes luminous with hatred.

Sealskins hung on the walls of the cave.

Dozens of sealskins.

These people were silkies. Seal-people.

Duncan was in a cave full of seal-people... and he was a seal-hunter.

The silkies left their fires and gathered around Duncan. The cave was silent, save for the crackling of fires, and the dripping of water from Duncan and the stranger.

'Do you know who we are, Duncan?' asked the silkie man who had brought him there.

'You're silkies,' said Duncan.

'Yes, Duncan, we are.'

Duncan shivered twice as hard as before.

'Are you going to kill me?' he asked in a whisper.

'Maybe,' said the silkie man. 'Maybe.'

'We could kill you, Duncan. Perhaps we should kill you. But we know a few things about you. We know that although you've killed many seals, you've never killed a pup. For that reason, we'll give you this one chance. Come with me.'

Duncan was led out of the cave and into a smaller cave. A solitary fire burned here, and a terrible stench curdled the air. Lying on a sealskin was a silkie man.

The man was old and thin. There was a dreadful wound in his back, a gash surrounded by diseased and rotting skin.

Protruding from that wound was Duncan's knife.

'This is my father,' said the silkie man.

'I'm sorry,' said Duncan, his voice breaking. 'I'm so sorry.'

'Don't be sorry,' said the silkie man. 'Help him.'

'How?' asked Duncan.

'You did this wrong, so you can right it.'

'How?'

'Pull the knife out, and kiss the wound.'

It didn't make sense to Duncan; yet he had no choice. If there was a chance that it could work, he had to try.

Duncan knelt down beside the old silkie man. The stench was so powerful that it made him gag. The wound was foul, with dried blood caked around it and yellow liquid oozing from it.

He had to try.

Duncan reached out and took hold of his knife. Quickly and smoothly, he pulled it out.

The old man gasped in pain. Blood and foul liquid poured from the wound.

Duncan set his knife down on the floor.

Summoning his courage, he leaned forward and kissed the wound.

Duncan drew back and retched. The old silkie man jerked and thrashed about before falling still.

He turned and looked at Duncan. Colour filled his cheeks.

'Thank you, Duncan,' he said.

Soon after that, Duncan, the silkie man and his father returned to the grand cave. When the silkie folk saw them, they leapt to their feet and barked and howled their joy.

'You've done a good thing,' said the silkie man to Duncan.

'And bad things,' said Duncan. 'So many bad things. I see that now.'

The silkies invited Duncan to stay and feast with them, but he politely refused. Shrugging his shoulders, the silkie man led Duncan back the way they came. This time, Duncan took a deep breath before going beneath the water. The silkie man pulled him with powerful strokes and soon he was on the beach by his house, waving as the silkie man swam away.

Duncan ran to his house, closed the door behind him and before he even took off his wet clothes, he took a knife from his kitchen drawer. Kneeling before his fire, Duncan undid his shirt, put the knife to his hand and cut his palm. Pressing his bloody palm to his heart, he spoke these words.

'I, Duncan Mackinnon, swear that I shall never again harm a seal. Everything I do, for the rest of my days, will be to help the seals.'

Duncan was true to his oath. He stopped hunting seals, sold his house and moved to the Isle of Skye. There, he bought a house and a wee bit of land, opposite a skerry where seals gathered. Duncan spent the rest of his life protecting those seals, making sure no-one came near the skerry or hunted seals in those waters.

Duncan didn't make many friends on Skye, for he was

seen as a queer fellow. But he made plenty of friends among the silkies. He feasted and danced with them until he was too old to dance. When he died, seals took his spirit to the caves of their ancestors, where he was made welcome by their fires.[1]

---

1. *This story can be found in Duncan Williamson's* Tales Of The Seal People. *The book is a classic and a must-have for anyone interested in Scottish folklore. Duncan heard the story from a deer stalker in Argyll named Peter Munro.*

    Silkies aren't generally described as having pale skin. I added this element as it seemed to me that they wouldn't get much sun.

21

THE HOUSE OF RIDDLES

A band of warriors known as the Fianna once roved the wilds of Scotland and Ireland. Their leader was a wise, handsome and generous man named Finn MacCoull. Finn was father to the warrior-poet Ossian, and Finn's two closest friends were named Caoilte and Diarmuid.

Caoilte was old and grey-haired, yet he was the swiftest runner of the Fianna. Diarmuid was kind, charming and a deadly spear-fighter. The tales of the Fianna are legion; here is one of them.

Finn was out hunting one afternoon with Caoilte, Ossian and Diarmuid. The sky was blue, the birds were singing and the forest was fat with deer. To be hunting together on such a day was all that any of them would wish for.

As they walked along a riverside path, Finn spied ahead

of them a giant. The giant had a great fork over his shoulder, and skewered upon its prongs was a wild boar. He walked as if every step cost him more strength than he had to give. The only thing that kept him moving, it seemed, was a young girl who skipped along at his side, singing words of encouragement.

Finn smiled and said, 'I would love to know who those folk are.'

Diarmuid ran ahead to speak with them. As he neared them, the girl turned and saw him. She flicked her wrist and cast a veil of mist around the hunters.

A few moments later, the mist dispersed. Finn and his men hadn't moved, yet upon the riverbank ahead of them was a house which hadn't been there before.

Finn and Caoilte caught up to Diarmuid. The hunters approached the house, wary yet curious.

Two wells stood outside of it. Upon one sat a rough iron vessel, while upon the other sat a copper vessel. The door of the house was open, and in the doorway was an old, bent-backed man, waving them in.

The hunters glanced at one another, nodded and entered the house.

Fire-smoke lingered in the dark air. Once their eyes had adjusted to the gloom, the warriors saw these strange sights.

In one corner sat the giant, his head in his hands as if sleep were about to take him. The girl sat at his side, watching them with a mischievous smile upon her face. In another corner lay a black-faced ram, with blue horns and green hooves. Beside the fire sat a crone. She was so old that flaps of skin hung from her face, revealing sinew and bone beneath. Across the fire from the crone sat an old man with twelve eyes.

'Look at this!' said the man who had waved them in. 'The Fianna have honoured us by entering our hall, yet we haven't offered them food. Shame upon us all!'

The girl leapt up and prodded the giant. 'Get up!' she said. 'Make a meal for Finn and his men!'

'Typical!' said the giant as he got to his feet. 'Do this, do that. Who does anything for me?' He went on grumbling as he took a knife from his belt and skinned the boar.

The Fianna were offered chairs. They sat and waited as the giant made a stew. The company sat in silence until the meal was ready and the girl went round with bowls for everyone.

As soon as they began eating, the ram leapt to its feet. It ran at Finn, seized his bowl between its teeth and took the bowl to its corner.

'Ha!' said the doorkeeper. 'Would you look at that! The mighty Finn MacCoull, his supper stolen by a sheep!'

'Stay there, father,' said Ossian. 'I shall retrieve your supper for you.' He put his bowl aside, rose to his feet and approached the ram. The ram rose to its feet too.

They eyed one another.

The ram gave a low, menacing bleat.

Ossian ran at the ram and grabbed its horns. It tossed him into the air and slammed him down on the dirt floor.

Shame-faced, Ossian returned to his seat. Diarmuid stood and went to face the ram.

The ram bleated at him. Its hooves scraped the floor.

Diarmuid leapt at the ram. He was a better fighter than Ossian; he lasted a few moments longer than his friend before the ram floored him. It gave a merry bleat and did a little skipping dance while the giant chuckled.

Caoilte went next. His fate was the same. He retreated to his chair, shame-faced.

Finally, Finn faced the ram.

He seized its horns. He gripped tightly.

The ram tried to twist. Finn resisted, his veins bulging as he pushed it back. He had never fought an enemy so strong.

The room spun around Finn and he crashed down on his back.

The inhabitants of the house laughed uproariously. The twelve-eyed man got to his feet. He went to the ram, took hold of its horns and led it back to its bed of straw.

'Shame!' said Caoilte. 'You laugh, when you should be ashamed of yourselves. None of you have offered Finn a drink.'

'That's true, said the doorkeeper. 'Go outside to the wells, please, Caoilte. They are sacred wells, and Finn may have a drink from whichever one you choose.'

Caoilte went outside and filled the copper vessel. He

brought it back inside and offered it to Finn. Finn was thirsty. He gulped the water down, moaning and shivering with delight as he drank. Neither food nor drink, poetry nor battle had ever given him so much pleasure as the liquid in the copper vessel.

'That,' he said as he lowered the cup from his lips, 'is the finest drink I ever tasted. What is...'

Finn said no more. He fell from his chair to the ground, heaving and shuddering. His eyes went red as he foamed at the mouth; he clawed at the air as if demons were tearing him apart from the inside.

'What's happening?' asked Diarmuid.

'I think he needs another drink,' said the doorkeeper.

Diarmuid understood. He ran outside, filled the rough iron vessel, returned and put it to Finn's lips. Finn grabbed the vessel, gulped and wretched. The liquid was so foul that it took all his will to drink it.

A few moments later, the iron cup fell from Finn's hands. He was himself again.

Finn got to his feet, and so did the old woman.

She took her shawl from over her shoulders and cast it at the Fianna. It grew in size and settled upon them. They sank to the floor, suddenly too tired to stand.

The cloak disappeared like mist while the proud warriors watched themselves age. Helpless upon the dirt floor, their muscles shrank and their skin wrinkled. They were ageing fast, and Finn found himself forgetting things.

Why had he come here? Who was he? What was the name of his son?

The only thing Finn knew for sure was that he was afraid; more afraid than he had ever been before.

'Come here, old warrior,' said the doorkeeper, 'and rest your head on my lap.'

Not knowing what else to do, Finn crawled slowly and painfully to where the doorkeeper sat and rested his head in the the man's lap.

'Don't worry,' said the doorkeeper, stroking Finn's thinning hair and spotted scalp. 'All is well.'

At that moment, the hag waved her hands and the warriors' strength and youth returned to them. They leapt to their feet and drew their swords.

'There is no need for weapons,' said the doorkeeper. 'Our game is at an end. Would you care to know the answers to these riddles, Finn?'

'I would,' said Finn, through gritted teeth.

'That giant,' said the doorkeeper, 'is sluggishness. Sluggishness, helped on by liveliness.' He indicated the girl. 'Both live in the hearts of all men.'

'What is the ram?' asked Caoilte.

'The ram is life.' He pointed at the twelve-eyed man. 'Life, which can only be overcome by death.'

'What were those liquids Finn drank?' asked Diarmuid.

'The copper vessel contains lies,' answered the doorkeeper, 'which taste sweet when they are told, but foul afterwards. In the iron vessel is truth; hard to swallow, yet better after.'

'What about the old woman?' asked Ossian.

'The old woman is old age. You are young and strong, poet, but she shall come for you in time.'

'And you?' asked Finn.

'That is a riddle for another day.'

Finn and his companions wished to press the man; yet a mist fell, and when it arose, the house was gone. The warriors made camp many miles away that night, and none of them slept easily.[1]

---

1. *I took this story from Lady Gregory's* Irish Myths and Legends. *Though it comes from an Irish collection, the Fianna stories were very much a shared currency between Scotland and Ireland.*

    There are many stories of Finn and his men arriving at a strange house and passing the night there, during which time their strength and wits are tested. These stories can be compared to accounts of shamans sending their spirits to other planes of reality, where they are made to face similar tests in order to gain knowledge and power.

    A closely related story can be found in David Campbell's Out Of The Mouth Of The Morning. *In this story, a young woman gives Diarmuid a spot upon his forehead which causes every woman who sees it to fall in love with him. This sets in course the events of* Diarmuid & Grainne, *the central story of the Fianna cycle.*

22

THE KNIGHT OF THE RED SHIELD

Finn MacCoull and a band of his men once went to Jura, the Isle of Deer, to hunt the red deer. They hunted all day before making their camp on the slopes of Beinn An Oir.

Meat stewed over campfires beneath a phoenix sky. The hunters sat around the fires with their hounds at their sides, the fading sunlight spinning the grass to gold.

'All is well with the Fianna,' said Caoilte. 'We are the mightiest company of men in the world. There isn't a person alive who could harm Finn here and now, with us surrounding him.'

An awkward silence followed this; then something curious happened.

The Fianna saw a ship of blazing fire sailing into Jura from the west. It docked in the bay, and from its prow leapt a warrior in black armour. He ran up the hill, taking such powerful strides that within a few moments he was standing before them.

Before anyone could say anything, he smacked Finn in the mouth, so hard that three of Finn's teeth fell out. The warrior picked up the teeth, turned and ran down the hill. He leapt into his blazing boat and sailed away.

Everyone glared at Caoilte.

'Maybe I was wrong,' said Caoilte. 'But no matter. I will follow that scoundrel, slaughter him and bring back Finn's teeth.'

'And I will go with him,' said bald-headed Conan, who didn't like Caoilte much but was in the mood for an adventure and a fight.

The two ageing warriors armed themselves, said their goodbyes and made their way downhill and through the bogs to the coast.

On their way, they heard a noise behind them. They turned to see Oscar, Finn's golden-haired grandson, running to catch up. Neither man wanted Oscar to join them. He was so young and achingly handsome that he made them feel even older and surlier than they were.

'Go back and see to your grandfather,' said Caoilte.

'I'd rather go adventuring,' said Oscar.

'We'd rather you stayed here,' said Conan.

'Try and make me,' said Oscar.

Caoilte was swift and strong despite his years. He seized

Oscar, carried him to the top of the mountain and tied him to it.

They set off again and soon heard another noise behind them. Turning, they saw Oscar with the crag still tied to his back. He had pulled it loose from the mountain.

'I'm coming with you,' he said, and this time they agreed.

After untying Oscar, the warriors carried on their way. They reached the coast and boarded their ship. The sails were hoisted, they spoke a prayer for good wind and soon they were sailing west, following a trail of smoke that rose from the black warrior's ship.

For three days and nights they followed the trail. On the fourth morning, Caoilte climbed the mast to see what could be seen, but fell down before reaching the top.

'Old fool,' laughed Conan. 'This is how it's done.' He heaved himself up, his knotted muscles bulging beneath his leathery skin, and fell down before he was halfway up.

'I'll take a look,' said Oscar.

He shinnied up the mast and called out, 'I see an island ahead. Upon the beach is a wall of flame, and it goes all the way around the island.'

'No wall of flame will stop us,' said Conan as Oscar climbed down the mast, to which Caoilte agreed. They brought the ship in, leapt onto the beach and approached the wall of flame.

'Right,' said Conan. 'Watch this.'

Conan charged at the flame-wall, roaring a battle-cry. He leapt into the air and fell short, landing among the flames. Howling, he ran from the flame-wall and rolled in the sand to put out the flames on his back.

'I'll show you how it's done,' said Caoilte.

The fast-footed warrior ran and leapt at the flame-wall. He met the same fate.

'I'll have a go,' said Oscar.

Oscar was younger and sprier than Conan and Caoilte, and he had learnt the salmon-leap from Diarmuid. He sailed over the flame-wall and landing with a flourish on the far side.

'Stay there and wait for me, but don't get too comfortable!' he called out. 'It won't take me long to find my grandfather's teeth.'

Beyond the ring of fire was a country of forests and mountains, where the grass was blue, the sky was green and the rocks were as clear as glass.

Oscar walked here and there until he came to the foot of a mountain. He heard a great roaring and rumbling sound, as if the mountain were clearing its throat. The sound was coming from somewhere up the mountain. Oscar was curious as to its source, so he began climbing.

Beneath the mountain's snowy peak, he saw a maiden sitting on the rocks. An ogre lay sleeping with his head in her lap. The maiden had dusky hair and sea-green eyes; she was more beautiful than fox-fur and the first geese of autumn.

'If you didn't have that big lad upon you, I would lay you down upon the rocks and kiss you,' said Oscar.

'If I didn't have this big lad upon me, I would lay you down and do more than kiss you,' said the girl.

'What can I do to wake him?' asked Oscar.

'Try cutting off his pinkie finger.'

Oscar drew his knife and cut off the ogre's pinkie. The ogre merely mumbled some curses and went back to snoring.

'I don't know what else to say,' said the maiden. 'No-one has ever managed to wake him. Some say he won't awaken until the Warrior of the Red Shield strikes a mountaintop against his chest.'

Oscar had never been called the Warrior of the Red Shield, but blood had soaked his shield in many a battle. He climbed up to the very tip of the mountain, pulled it loose, brought it back down and plunged it into the ogre's heart.

The ogre's eyes opened. He reached for Oscar, but as he did so, blood poured from his mouth. The ogre rolled from the maiden's lap onto the rocks. He was dead.

'There,' said Oscar. 'Now, let's see what this lad has about him.' He looked through the ogre's pouches and found three teeth.

'Finn's teeth!' said Oscar.

He pocketed the teeth and kissed the maiden. Sometime later, he announced it was time from him to return to his ship.

'I'll come with you,' said the maiden.

'I'd like that,' said Oscar.

They climbed down the hill and walked until they reached the flame-wall. Oscar salmon-leaped over it with the maiden in his arms. Caoilte and Oscar were sitting on the beach, gaming with a board they had drawn upon the sand.

'Entertain my bride,' said Oscar to Caoilte and Conan. 'This is a fine place, and I imagine there's more fighting and adventuring to be done here.'

The maiden sat down to game with Caoilte and Conan. Oscar leapt over the flame-wall and was gone.

This time, Oscar followed a road that led west through forests and glens to a seaside village. Three men were camped at the roadside just outside the village, sharpening their swords.

'What is this place, and who are you?' asked Oscar.

'We are fighting men,' said the first of them. 'Beyond the village, between the land and sea, is a battlefield. Every day, we do battle there with one hundred servants of the Son of Darkness, Son of Dimness. Every day we defeat them, but in the morning they rise up again, as strong as they ever were.'

'Let's get some food and drink,' said Oscar, 'and share stories tonight. In the morning, I will join you on the battlefield.'

'We are under spells,' said the second man, 'that none may join us in battle.'

'Then stay in bed tomorrow,' said Oscar. 'I will face them alone.'

Oscar and the fighting men entered the village together. They took a table in the inn and caroused through the night, telling stories and singing songs that have gone from the world now.

At last, the three drunken warriors returned to their camp. Oscar went out into the red dawn.

He came to the beach. It was easy to spot; it was strewn with bodies, the sky thick with kites and crows. Oscar sat on a rock and waited until the sun rose out of the mouth of the morning.

In that moment, fingers twitched. Mouths groaned, sword-arms flexed and a hundred bloodied corpses rose from death. Those with eyes fixed them on Oscar, who drew his sword and shouted his battle-cry.

The ghouls fought well; they were quick and cunning. Oscar battled them all day, iron ringing on iron, their savage shrieks never ceasing. Oscar nearly became a corpse himself many times, but his skills won out. Come sunset, he stood alone upon the blood-drenched sand.

That was when the Son of Darkness, Son of Dimness strode through the flame-wall.

This wasn't the warrior who had knocked out Finn's teeth; but he looked almost as fearsome. Wearily, Oscar drew his sword again.

Laughing and dancing, spinning and leaping, the Son of Darkness came at Oscar. Black as a kelpie's dreams were his armour, his hair and his eyes. Oscar battled him for hours, and it was the hardest fight Oscar ever fought. At last, Oscar triumphed and sliced off his enemy's head.

Oscar took his enemy's spear and fell to the sand. His death-dealing was finished, and so was he; he couldn't even crawl back to his friends. Oscar fell asleep amid those he had slaughtered.

He awoke at dawn, just as something else came through the flame-wall.

An old, serpentine woman slithered up the sand. She had no legs; instead she had a fat tail, like a slug or a grey snake. She wore a dress of bones and rotting skins; a tooth as long as a walking stick grew from her right palm.

The hag went to the first corpse, bent over it and put a finger in its mouth. The moment she did so, it came to life.

She went to the next corpse, and the next, doing the same. The corpses rose up again.

Oscar played dead until she came to him. When she put

her finger in his mouth, he licked it, just to startle her, before biting it off.

The hag screamed. She slapped him so hard that he flew over seven hills before crashing down on a bare hillside. She raced over the hills and found him there.

'Wretched worm,' she said. 'I will make a gown of your entrails.'

She lunged at him with her long tooth. Oscar leapt back, narrowly avoiding its point. He aimed at her the spear he had stolen from the Son of Darkness, Son of Dimness.

'That is my son's weapon,' she hissed.

'And I promise to look after it,' said Oscar. He threw it so hard that it went into her heart, out of her back and nailed her to a tree.

Oscar collapsed again.

Later that day, the three fighting men came looking for Oscar and found him.

'Thank you for coming,' said Oscar, 'but I think this is my end.'

'Not so,' said the first of the men. 'It is known that the hag, the mother of the Son of Darkness, carries a healing balm which cures any wounds given by her or her son.'

He went to the hag's body, searched through the pockets

of the skins she wore and found the jar of balm, which he rubbed on Oscar's wounds.

The four of them went back to the inn. They shared songs and stories again, and the following day, they walked up to a high hilltop to play shinty and clear their heads. As they sported in the sunshine, they looked out to sea and saw a ship of blazing flames coming towards the island.

Oscar knew that ship.

He dropped his shinty stick and drew his sword.

The blazing ship docked and the warrior who had taken Finn's teeth leapt through the flame-wall.

'He is the one who took my grandfather's teeth,' said Oscar.

'That is the Great Son of the Sons of the Universe,' said one of the fighting men.

The three of them dropped their sticks and fled.

The Great Son bounded through the flame-wall and up through the hills towards Oscar. Flames billowed about him and he sucked the light from the sky with his breath.

The Great Son of the Sons of the Universe landed before Oscar. He drew his blazing sword from its scabbard.

'You will be looking for your doting grandfather's teeth, Oscar,' said the Great Son of the Sons of the Universe.

'I already have them,' said Oscar.

'Ha! Foolish Fianna,' laughed the Great Son. 'Those are horse's teeth you took from the ogre. I have Finn's teeth, and you must fight me to get them back.'

If Oscar was ever afraid to fight anyone, it was the Great Son of the Sons of the Universe. Despite his fear, he didn't hesitate. He raised his sword and charged at his enemy.

They fought from hillside to shore to mountaintop, the Great Son drawing daylight and starlight and every nightmare ever dreamed into his blade. The world ended and began again as they fought, and Oscar could see no hope of winning.

'Come, Oscar!' cried the Great Son of the Sons of the Universe. 'I expected a better fight than this. The Fianna are said to fight like bears; you fight like a sickly sparrow.'

Oscar growled and changed tactics.

Instead of striking one, he struck twice. He rained volley after volley of blows upon his enemy. Every last stroke he made, he made at the ground beneath him.

Oscar was ready. He moved back, opening his guard.

The Great Son roared and ran at him.

He fell into the hole Oscar had dug.

With a mighty swing, Oscar severed the head of the Great Son of the Sons of the Universe. The Great Son fell down dead, his fires extinguished, and Oscar took from his pouch Finn's teeth.

Oscar was tired of the island and ready to go home. He returned to the flame-wall, leapt over it and found that Conan, Caoilte and the maiden had left. Their boat was nowhere to be seen.

'I have been betrayed,' said Oscar.

He returned to the village and sought out his three friends. They apologised for not staying by his side, and offered to provide him with a boat, along with three pigeons to guide him home. Oscar accepted, and he set sail for Scotland.

Days later, Oscar arrived at Finn's hall in Glen Lyon.

He entered the hall. Dozens of warriors sat feasting at the tables. Finn was sitting in his high seat.

Oscar's eyes roved the hall and found Caoilte and Conan. The maiden from the mountaintop sat at Conan's side.

'Oscar,' called Conan as the hall fell quiet. 'You have a nerve showing your face here, after you ran from the battle in which we took back Finn's teeth.'

There was a dark muttering, and much glaring at Oscar.

Oscar approached Finn.

'Did Caoilte and Conan return your teeth to you?' he asked.

'Yes,' said Finn, 'but they don't fit well. I have taken to hammering them in each evening, which pains me greatly.'

'Take them out,' said Oscar.

Finn took out the teeth, which were the horse's teeth which Oscar had taken from the ogre's pouch. Oscar took the real teeth from his own pouch, dropped them in a cup of ale and offered it to Finn.

Finn drank the ale, and the three teeth put themselves back into place.

Oscar turned to the company and told his story. When he was done, it was agreed that the Fianna would feast in Oscar's name for three weeks, while Caoilte and Conan washed dishes in the kitchen.[1]

---

1. *I found a version of this story in J.F. Campbell's* Popular Tales Of The West Highlands. *The protagonists of this story are not members of the Fianna, but in the notes, Campbell mentions a very similar story in which they are. I took the story given in the text, populated it with characters from the Fianna cycle and added in some details. The island with the ring of fire around it may refer to Iceland.*

23

THE KING OF NORWAY'S BROWN HORSE

There once lived near Inverness a wealthy farmer named Conall, who had three sons. His sons did everything together and loved to go out fishing, hunting and exploring in the forests and glens.

One day in summer, they left the house to go swimming in a waterfall pool. They made their way down the road and through the woods until they heard the waterfall's roar. Reaching the pool, they dived, swam and sported in the sunshine.

As they swam, they saw three other young men approach the pool. The young men wore fine clothes and had a haughty look about them.

'You there,' said the eldest of the three. 'Get out of the pool. We have come here to swim, and we want the pool to ourselves.'

'Why should we, when we were here first?' said Conall's eldest son, whose name was Aidan.

'Because we are the King's sons.'

'I don't care whose sons you are,' said Aidan. 'There's plenty of room here for everyone. You can swim with us, or wait until we are finished, or fight us.'

'We'll fight you,' said the King's eldest son.

Silence fell. Conall's sons climbed out the water, dressed themselves and faced the King's sons. They knew how to fight, but the King's sons looked strong and unafraid.

With shouts and howls the boys clashed. Conall's youngest son brought his opponent down with a punch. The two middle sons wrestled; soon Conall's middle son had his opponent pinned on the grass. Aidan's opponent was tougher. The two eldest sons went on fighting until they were both bleeding and soaked with sweat.

They fought on the grass, on the stony bank and in the water. Here their struggling grew desperate, and the other boys all shouted for them to stop. Yet neither would stop, for fear that the other would not.

They got to their feet and exchanged punches. Aidan caught the King's son with a blow that made his nose spout blood.

Howling, the King's son reached down and grabbed a rock.

He swung it at Aidan's head. Aidan leaned back, evading the rock.

The King's son slipped and fell forward. There was a cracking sound as his head struck a rock.

The boy's brothers began to scream. They dragged their brother onto the bank. He stared up at them, unblinking, as blood seeped into the sand.

The King's eldest son was dead.

Conall's sons ran for home. They told their father what had happened.

'This is a bad business,' he said. 'I will need to see the King, and hope he is merciful; or he will not be the only one to lose a son.'

Conall left the house the next day. He rode for the King's castle and was given admittance. Soon, he was standing before the throne.

'It was my sons that your sons met at the pool,' said Conall. 'I am deeply sorry for the loss of your heir. Yet, my sons tell me it was your sons who started the fight.'

'I am not interested in who started the fight,' said the King. 'My firstborn is dead, and his life must be paid for.'

Conall tried to keep his face expressionless as he listened.

'Having said that,' said the King, 'there is no profit for me in killing your son. Doing so would not bring mine back. Yet, there is something that would recompense me for his death.

'You have surely heard that I am a lover of fine horses. The King of Norway has a chestnut-brown stallion. They say it runs faster than the wind; faster than love's madness strikes the heart; faster than a woman's mind. I have long coveted it, and now I wish for you, Conall, to bring me the stallion. If you do not, the price you pay for my son's death shall be a blood-price.'

Conall walked home slowly and wearily. How he could he ever hope to steal a horse from the King of Norway? He had to try. Conall reached home and told his wife and his sons what had happened. A few days later, he and his sons sailed for Norway.

After a long crossing, they finally spied the Norwegian fjords and the harbour of Bergen. They docked their ship and took a table in a tavern, where they quietly discussed their next move.

'What I fancy we should do,' said Conall, 'is to find the house of the King's miller.'

A few casual questions and a few coins worked their charm, and that evening they arrived at the house they sought. The miller was surprised by his unexpected visitors, but he invited them in. Conall plied him with whisky, and in the slow hours of night, he told their tale.

'I have coin,' said Conall, 'and will pay for any help you can give me.'

The miller sipped his whisky as he thought over what Conall had said.

'I think I can help you,' he said. 'It will not be easy, and you will likely be caught. The King is a hard man, but a fair man, and he has always treated me well. Yet your sons do not deserve death, so I will help you.

'I will put you in sacks,' continued the miller, 'and deliver you to the King's stables. You will have to get the horse out without being heard and bring it here. If you can get it here, I can hide it until you leave.'

Conall agreed to the plan.

The following evening, the miller drove his cart to the King's hall and around to the stables. He was well-known, and no-one thought to check his sacks. He and his gillie, whom he trusted well, unloaded the sacks in the stables before leaving the way they came.

A short while later, Conall and his sons crawled out of their sacks and looked around. The stables were lit by by low lamps. A dozen horses stood in the stalls, and in a stall at the rear of the stable was a magnificent brown stallion, which eyed them warily.

'That must be it!' said Aidan.

Before he could move, Conall put a hand on Aidan's shoulder. 'Not yet,' he whispered. 'We must make a hiding place, in case we are discovered.'

They found a spade and took turns digging in the corner

of an empty stable, until they had made a hole big enough to fit them all.

'If there's trouble, we'll climb in here and cover the hole up with straw,' said Conall.

Now that their hiding place was ready, it was time to approach the stallion.

Conall made the boys wait behind him while he approached it. He had reared many horses, and knew their ways. Slowly he walked towards the stallion, speaking in a voice as soft as fawn-skin. When he came close, the stallion gave a great whinny and drummed its hooves upon the stable door.

The King of Norway looked up from his meal.

He was sitting at his table, surrounded by his family, his friends and his serving men. The King beckoned to a serving man and said, 'I heard my brown stallion whinny. Send some guards to the stables and have them see that everything is in order.'

The guards entered the stables. They saw nothing amiss, and reported back to the King.

Conall and his sons emerged from their hiding place.

'We shall wait a while and try again,' said Conall.

After some time had passed, Conall once more approached the stallion. He fared no better; the stallion neighed and drummed its hooves on the stable door.

The King had gone to bed by this point. He called for his

guards, and had them check the stables again, but they found nothing amiss.

Later that night, Conall and his sons emerged from their hiding hole again.

A third time, Conall approached the stallion, using all his patience and skill. The stallion only neighed louder and drummed its hooves more furiously.

The King shot up in bed. 'That does it,' he said. 'Someone is in the stables, and I will find him.'

He dressed, gathered his guards and went out to the stables. This time, he ordered the guards to search every inch of the building until they found the intruder. Conall and his sons were discovered and pulled from their hiding hole.

'You are not men of Norway,' said the King.

'My name is Conall,' said Conall. 'These are my sons, and we are Scotsmen.'

The King spoke Gaelic. As angry as he was to find the Scotsmen in his stables, he was intrigued too.

'Bring them to my throne room,' he ordered his guards, 'and I will hear their tale.'

In the King's hall, fires burned in a dozen braziers, reflecting off the shields that adorned the walls. The King's chief serving man had been roused from sleep. He attended to the

King, who sat on his throne, looking down at his prisoners and stroking his beard.

'So,' said the King, 'tell me your tale.'

Conall did so, from the fight at the waterfall pool to the moment they were caught.

The King leaned back on his throne.

'If I were you,' he said, 'I would have done as you have done. But I am not you, and no man has crossed me and lived to tell of it. The penalty for your actions is death.' He signalled for mead to be poured. 'Yet I admire your daring, and I am a sporting man. So I will say this.

'If you, Conall, can tell me of a time when you were in harder straits than this, tell me of it now. If I am impressed by your tale, I will let one of your sons go.'

'I can tell you of such a time, sire,' said Conall without hesitation.

He cleared his throat and began his story.

When I was a young man, my father kept a herd of cows. One day, he came home and told me that one of the cows had calved, and that I was to go and fetch it.

I set off in the afternoon, with a younger lad who was helping us on the farm. The herd had roamed some distance, and we walked through forests and over moors until we found them.

We led the calf back the way we came. As we walked, the wind began to sing. Clouds massed above us; rain fell, and then snow.

'There's a bothy in those woods,' I said to the lad. 'We'll take shelter and wait for the storm to pass.'

We found the bothy, and were glad to see that the last occupant had left a stack of firewood. Soon we had a fire blazing, and we hung our cloaks up to dry.

I hadn't expected the storm to last long, but it did. We waited it out, being in no hurry and thinking now to pass the night in the bothy. Day turned to night, the hours creaked by, and in the depths of the night, we heard a noise outside.

The door to the bothy opened.

Into the bothy came a group of eleven wildcats. They were bigger than any cats you've ever seen, as big as dogs; and their leader was even bigger, as big as a wild boar. He had one eye and red fur like a fox.

He looked us over and said, 'Thank you, Conall, for sharing your bothy with us.'

'It's not my bothy,' I said.

'We are bards,' the big, one-eyed cat went on. 'We are known among cats as the finest singers of our kind. No doubt, you would like to hear us.'

'Well, yes,' I said, 'I suppose so... I mean, it's fine if you don't want to...'

He turned to the other cats. 'Sing for Conall!' he said.

At once, the other cats struck up a song. I've been west

and I've been east in my time, and I swear I never heard a worse sound than that song.

Finally, they finished. At once, the big cat turned to me and said, 'We'll be needing payment, Conall. We'll be needing payment for the song.'

'Payment? I've no money on me.'

'Well, then,' said the cat, 'we'll take your calf instead.'

Before I could speak, they leapt upon the calf. The poor thing bleated for its mother, but the big cat silenced it by ripping out its throat. The cats ate and ate until there was nothing left of it but bones.

The one-eyed cat turned to me again, licking blood from its lips.

'Time for another song, eh, Conall?' he said.

I opened my mouth to say I didn't want a song; but they had already begun. This song was as bad as their last song, and when they had finished, the big cat said to me, 'Time for payment, Conall.'

'But I've no money, I told you, and no calf now either. There's just me and the lad...'

They fell upon the lad. He squealed like a speared pig and was soon silenced. I closed my eyes and covered my ears as they tore his flesh and gulped down his gizzards. I realised that once they were finished, they would surely sing again, and demand payment again. The only payment I had left to offer was myself.

I leapt up and ran out of the door.

Into the woods, I dashed. The moon shone out from among the racing clouds. The wildcats were after me now, I could hear them miaowing and yowling; but I was always a good tree-climber. Stopping below a tree, I leapt up and caught the lowest branch. I pulled myself up and climbed until I was high above the forest floor. It was winter, so the branches were bare; I could only pray that the cats wouldn't look up and spot me.

I watched. I waited. Soon enough, the cats appeared beneath my tree. I watched them pace back and forth, sniffing the air; thankfully the snow was still falling and had obscured my footprints.

I was just beginning to think myself safe when the big cat appeared.

Sniffing the air, he came to the bottom of my tree and looked up, right into my eyes.

He miaowed. The other cats came running and he cried, 'Up the tree! Up the tree and bring him down to me!'

At once, a cat leapt up, sunk its claws into the tree-trunk and began to climb. When it came close, I kicked out, struck it on the head and sent it tumbling to the ground.

Another cat came; the same thing happened. After I had sent a third cat flying, the big cat said, 'Dig up the roots! Bring the tree down!'

The cats surrounded the tree and began digging. It wasn't

a huge tree, and the cats were strong. Soon they exposed the roots.

They dug up a first root. The tree shook. As it shook, I gave out a cry, for now I was sure that they had me.

Nearby, unbeknownst to me, a warrior band sat around a campfire.

One of them heard my shout. He said to the others, 'Someone is in trouble. We should go and help him.'

'You're imagining things,' said the leader of the band, a grizzled old warrior. 'Sit back down.' So he did.

The cats dug up a second root. The tree swung wildly, and I cried out again.

At the camp, another man stood up. 'Someone is in trouble, we must go and help him,' he said. The leader ordered him to sit down.

The cats dug away, scrabbling madly in the dirt. They brought a third root to the surface, and again the tree swung back and forth. The cats howled and yowled, watching the tree swing, and I gave out a cry as it came crashing to the forest floor.

The leader of the warriors leapt up and drew his sword. 'I heard it that time,' he said. 'Someone is in trouble, and we shall help!'

I got to my feet. The cats surrounded me.

They tensed, ready to leap.

In that instant, the warriors came charging towards the cats. I watched, helpless, as each of the men engaged a cat in battle. They were armed with swords and spears, and knew how to use them; but the cats were quick and cunning, and armed with sharp claws and teeth.

The battle raged on. Men and cats fell bleeding to the ground.

Finally, there were only two left.

The leader of the men faced the big one-eyed cat. Daylight crept into the forest as they fought, their skills evenly matched, their battle both terrible and wondrous.

Finally, the old warrior skewered the cat with his spear. The cat fell down dead, and the warrior fell down dead on top of it.

The calf, the lad, the cats and the warriors all died that night. I was the only one who survived. And being up that tree, as it swayed back and forth, with the cats beneath me, thirsty for my blood; that was a worse situation than I am in now.

The King laughed and stood up to stretch.

'A fine tale indeed, Conall,' said the King. 'I am true to my word. With that tale, you have saved your eldest son from the noose.'

'Thank you, sire,' said Conall, with a bow and a great sigh of relief.

'Such a tale,' said the King. 'I find myself wondering.

Could you have ever been in worse straits than you were that night, up the tree, with the cats howling for your blood? I think not. But if you were, I would hear of it; and you might just buy the life of your second son.'

'There was a time when I was in worse straits than that, sire,' said Conall.

'Then take a cup of mead,' said the King. His serving man brought mead for Conall and his sons. Conall drank a deep draught, cleared his throat and began again.

My father's lands lay by the sea. On the days when I was released from work, I liked nothing better than to stroll along the shore and explore the beaches, cliffs and caves.

I went out one day beneath a dark cloak of storm clouds. Storms didn't trouble me; I loved to watch towering waves strike the shore while the black sky hurled its spears at the sea.

As I walked along a clifftop that day, a gust of wind knocked me from my feet and into a gap between the rocks.

I tumbled, not to my death, but into a pile of dung. As my head spun, I looked around and saw I was in a cave. Great heaps of dung lined the cave, and among them wandered a herd of two dozen goats. By a fire, blocking the entrance to the cave, sat a giant. One of his eyes was crusted over with scabs; his other eye was fixed on me.

'Conall,' said the giant. 'I am glad you came to visit. My knife has long been rusting in its sheath, waiting to taste your tender flesh.'

'My flesh is tender enough,' I said, 'but I have better gifts to offer you than the taste of my flesh.'

'Like what?' said the giant.

'I am a druid,' I said, 'and I can restore sight to that eye of yours. I only ask that if I succeed, you let me go.'

'Very well,' said the giant.

I climbed out of the manure and asked the giant to heat water in his cauldron. As the water warmed, I waved my hands over it, muttering words which I pretended were spells. When the water was boiled, I took a sprig of heather from my pack, dipped it in the water and climbed onto the giant's knee.

'Bend down,' I said. He leant forward and I began to rub the heather against his good eye.

'That hurts!' he said. 'What are you doing?'

'Hold still,' I said. 'I'm taking sight from the good eye to give to the bad eye.'

The giant clenched his teeth as I rubbed harder with the heather. When I judged my work to be done, I leapt down from the giant's knee and ran to a corner of the cave.

'Why have you stopped?' he cried out. 'Get back here and...'

The giant realised what I'd done. I'd ruined his good eye, and now he was totally blind.

He roared his fury, but didn't leave the cave mouth as I'd hoped he would.

'You think you are clever, Conall,' he said. 'But you will not leave this place alive.'

For the rest of that day and all that night, the giant sat with his back to the cave mouth. I thought about trying to squeeze past him, but it was too risky; so I bided my time and waited for my chance.

My chance came the next morning.

The giant awoke and said, 'I will let my goats out now, Conall. You might be thinking you will slip out among them, but I will feel the shape of them as they pass, so there is no chance you shall escape.'

The giant did as he said, getting up and making way for the goats to pass. They lined up to leave the cave, and as each goat passed him, he examined it with his hands, ensuring that it was a goat, and not me, that left his cave.

I crept up behind one of the goats. I wrapped my hand around its mouth and cut its throat. Working faster than I had ever worked, I skinned the goat and put the skin on my back. I wrapped the skin of its hind legs around my legs; I wrapped the skin of its forelegs around my arms. With my mouth in its mouth, its nose upon my nose, I dropped to all fours and walked towards the cave mouth.

The giant lay his hands upon me. He squeezed and prodded me.

He let me pass.

Out onto the sand and into the eagle-light of dawn I went. Laughing, I threw off my disguise, turned and shouted to the giant.

'You are not as clever as you think, giant,' I said. 'For I have escaped your cave.'

The giant came lumbering out of the cave. I backed away; I wouldn't let him get close.

He laughed. 'Very well, Conall. I will admit it; you are wiser than I am. You have been good sport. Let me give you a gift before you go.'

He reached into his pocket and took out a golden ring.

'Please accept this, Conall,' he said, and threw it onto the sand.

I was wary of accepting a gift from him; but I'd never owned a ring before, let alone a ring of gold. Keeping my eyes on the giant, I walked to the ring and picked it up. It shone in the sunlight and I was entranced.

I put it upon my finger.

At once, the ring began to scream.

'He's here!' it screamed. 'Conall is here!'

The giant bounded across the sand in my direction. I turned and ran as fast I could, making for a path that led up to the clifftops, the ring shouting and screaming on my finger. I tried to pull it off but it was stuck.

Up the path I dashed. It was a narrow one, and the giant had to squeeze between two cliff-faces to climb up it. I reached the top and raced over the cliffs, the giant gaining on me all the time.

Just in time, I reached the place I sought.

At the edge of a gap between two cliff ledges, I pulled my knife from its sheath. The giant was almost upon me.

The ring was on my left forefinger. I lay it out flat on a rock, grit my teeth and chopped it off with my knife. Dropping the knife, I grabbed my finger and threw it into the gap.

The ring went on shouting as it fell into the gap.

I leapt aside.

The giant ran past me and over the cliff.

When I looked into the gap, I saw him lying dead at the bottom.

'It is a hard, situation, sire,' said Conall, 'being your prisoner here, with my sons and I facing the gallows. It was harder still, up that tree, with the cats after my blood; and it was harder still, running from the giant, with his ring screaming upon my finger. A finger I no longer have.'

Conall raised a four-fingered hand.

The King chuckled. 'I would imagine so, Conall. You have saved your second son, and proved yourself to be silver-tongued. No better teller has graced my hall in many seasons.'

The door opened and the King's mother came in.

'I couldn't sleep. My maid said tales are being told,' she said. She looked at Conall. 'Am I too late, or will there be another?'

'Will there be another, Conall?' said the King. 'If you can tell me about a time when you were in even worse straits, I will release your third son.'

'There was such a time, sire,' said Conall.

The serving man filled their cups, and Conall embarked on his tale.

A few years after my meeting with the giant, I married and moved to Torridon. I hunted among the hills and fished in the lochs, and my hunting trips would sometimes last many days.

On one such trip, my wandering led me to a loch surrounded by pine-clad mountains. There was an island in the middle of the loch, and close to where I stood on the shore was a rowing boat.

I approached the boat and was astonished to find it full of treasures. Jewelled cups and rings lay on a bed of gold and silver coins.

'Did these treasures come from that island?' I asked myself. 'If so, what other wonders await there?'

I climbed into the boat. The moment I did so, the boat

started to move. It carried me all the way across the loch to the island.

The boat landed on a little beach on the island. There was nothing for it but to get out and go exploring. As soon as I left the boat, though, it took off, returning to the far shore and leaving me stranded on the island.

I walked here and there, seeing ash and rowan and birch trees, but nothing out of the ordinary; until I climbed a little hill.

There was a hole in the ground at the top of the hill. Smoke billowed through it. I got down on my knees and looked into the hole, and this is what I saw.

A young woman sat in a kitchen with a baby in her lap. The baby was laughing and smiling, and the woman held a knife.

She put the knife to the baby's throat.

I thought she would kill the baby; but it laughed and she lowered the knife, her shoulders sagging. She did this again and again, until she gave up, put down the knife and cried.

I called out to her. She looked up, startled, and asked who I was, and what I was doing there. I told her my tale, and learnt that she had arrived there the same way as me. She told me where I could find an entrance to the underground hall. I found it after some searching and joined her in the kitchen.

'A blind giant lives here,' she said. 'He will be back

tonight. He has ordered me to kill my baby and cook him, so that he can eat him.'

'You won't have to do that,' I told her. 'I'm no stranger to dealing with giants.'

I searched the giant's home, which was a labyrinth of winding stairs, chambers and corridors, reaching deep beneath the ground. Down in its depths, I smelt a dreadful stench. Following the stench, I came to a heavy oaken door.

I opened the door and found myself looking down on a vast hall full of naked corpses. The smell was dreadful, and the sight of all those dead eyes staring up at me was unnerving.

I returned to the young woman and suggested that we hide the baby, and feed the giant a corpse in its place.

'No good,' she said. 'Every evening he counts the corpses before he eats his supper. He will know if one is missing.'

'There's an easy answer to that,' I said.

We hid the baby, wrapping it up in blankets at the back of a cupboard. I dragged a dead infant up from the corpse-chamber and set it to cook in the giant's cauldron, before returning to the corpse chamber and lying down among the dead.

The giant came home. When the young woman fed him the corpse, he said, 'This meat is tough. It better not be one of my corpses.'

'Your corpses are in their chamber,' she replied. 'Go and count them if you like.'

'I will,' he said as he finished eating the child's corpse.

He made his way down to the corpse-chamber. Lying among the dead, I saw him enter. I lay still as his hands roved among the corpses.

'One, two, three... seventy-four, seventy-five...'

'They are all here,' he said to himself at last. 'I am still hungry, so I will have another before I go to bed.' He plucked me from the pile and carried me back to the kitchen.

'Cook this corpse for me,' he ordered his captive, dropping me into the cauldron.

She had no choice but to obey. The water had cooled, but she built up the fire beneath the cauldron until it was blazing. All too soon, the water was warming.

It got hotter. Hotter still. The heat was terrible, my skin was reddening and scalding. I thought this was surely the end of my adventures; but then the giant fell asleep, slumping to the floor by the cauldron.

The woman hauled me out of the water. Without waiting a moment, I grabbed my knife from its sheath and rammed it into the giant's left eye.

The giant roared, jumped to his feet and thrashed around. He smashed his kitchen to pieces as he sought his attacker. He would surely have caught us, had he not charged into the wall of the kitchen. The impact drove my knife through his eye and into his brain.

The giant fell down dead.

We cried for joy. The young woman retrieved her baby from its hiding place and cradled it in her arms.

In the morning, we left the giant's house. We found the boat waiting for us, and it took us back over the water.

When we landed, the young woman thanked me before disappearing into the forest, her baby in her arms. I never saw her again. And I can tell you, sire, that it is hard, the prospect of dying alongside my sons on the gallows. It was harder, being up that tree, with the cats baying for my blood. It was even harder, running from a giant, with his ring screaming on my finger; yet it was hardest of all to be cooking in a giant's cauldron.

Before the King could say anything, his mother spoke.

'That story you told just now. Is it one you heard and made your own, or did it truly happen to you?'

'On my oath,' said Conall, 'it happened to me, though it was many years go. This ring I wear,' he held up his hand, 'is one I took from the little rowing boat.'

The King's mother nodded. 'It was you,' she said with a smile. 'And it was me. I was the young woman whom you rescued from the giant's island. The boy you saved was my son, who sits before you.'

Conall stared at her, open-jawed. 'By my beard,' he said. 'I recognise you now.'

There was much laughter, more ale and more tales, until dawn and into the next evening. Conall and his sons were all spared the noose, and the King of Norway gave Conall his chestnut stallion, as thanks for saving his life all those years ago. Conall gave the stallion to his own king, and his debt was considered to have been paid.[1]

---

1. *This is another Campbell story. It is a fine example of the frame story, in which a group of stories are told within the framework of a larger story.* The Thousand And One Nights *is the best-known example of this, in which Sharhazad tells a story each night to delay her death, just as Conall does here. Frame stories provide a flexible structure for storytellers who can add or remove stories according to their preference.*

I suspect that this is a very old story, as it mirrors many processes of shamanic initiation. Conall ascends into the sky on his first adventure, and is saved from danger. On his second adventure, he enters an underworld. He shape-shifts by donning the goat skin, uses trickery to save himself and is dismembered. On Conall's third adventure, he enters another underworld. This time he dies and is reborn by lying among the corpses and being cooked in the cauldron. He saves not just himself but the young woman, her baby and ultimately his own sons.

You can hear me tell this story on House of Legends Podcast.

24

THE SNAKE SHIRT

Further east than East and further west than West, a castle once stood at the centre of a kingdom. Its black walls had never been breached, and its bristling turrets scraped the sky.

Within those walls lived the King, the Queen and the Prince. The King was old and grey-bearded, yet his crow-haired queen was young and voluptuous. Every bard in every tavern knew a hundred songs in praise of her beauty.

The Queen was not the Prince's mother; she was his step-mother. Sickness had stolen the Prince's mother, and the King had remarried a few years later. The Prince grieved his mother terribly, yet his stepmother was kind to him, never seeking to replace his mother in his heart, and for that he was grateful.

In those days, a boy ceased being a boy on his sixteenth

midsummer. On that day, he was called a man. The Prince's sixteenth midsummer drew near, and the King ordered that a feast be prepared.

The night of the feast came. From his chambers, the Prince watched as kings and queens, princes and princesses, lords and ladies rode in through the gates.

He turned to face his mirror. Was that a man looking back at him, he wondered, or a boy?

His father would send a servant to fetch him soon. He should be down in the feasting hall, greeting his guests. Instead he hid in his chamber, afraid to feel his guests' eyes upon him; watching him, judging him and finding him lacking. His father had fought in more wars than anyone could recall; he was feared and respected. The Prince, on the other hand, was clumsy in the saddle, and better with a set of pipes than a sword.

A knock sounded at the door.

The Queen entered. She wore a blood-red gown, and a ruby at her neck.

'Are you ready?' she asked.

He didn't answer.

'I know how you feel,' she said. 'It was hard for me to sit by your father's side when we married. All those people watching me, comparing me to your mother.'

'The people love you. They don't love me,' said the Prince.

'You will win their hearts. I know you compare yourself

to your father, but yours is a different strength.' She stepped forward. 'I brought you a gift.'

In her hands, she held a dark bundle of cloth. She handed it to him and he unfolded it. It was a silk shirt, finer than he had ever touched, crimson with black and gold embroidery.

'I had it made especially,' she said. 'Red for strength, black like your hair, gold like the crown you shall one day wear. Though not too soon, I hope,' she said with a laugh.

'It's beautiful,' he said.

'Put it on and join us downstairs,' she said before departing.

The Prince unbuttoned the shirt he wore and donned the silk shirt. It was tight, yet he loved the feel of it.

He looked in the mirror again. Yes. He looked more regal in this. More like a man.

He was ready.

If only the shirt wasn't so tight.

It seemed to feel tighter than it had a moment before. How could that be? Now it felt even tighter.

The shirt was shrinking.

The silk pressed against his ribs, squeezing him, making him gasp for breath. He had to get it off. The Prince grabbed at the shirt's top button; it was no longer there.

In horror, the Prince watched the black silk change, becoming scales that glittered in the candlelight. The shirt was moving on its own now, writhing, changing shape.

He looked in the mirror and would have screamed, had he the breath.

The shirt had become a black snake. Its coils were wrapped around his body and bunched in a mass upon his shoulders. The snake's eyes met his own as he stared at it in the mirror, its mouth open to reveal a forked tongue and glistening fangs.

He fell to his knees, gasping for breath.

Another knock sounded at the door.

'Your father ask that you come downstairs, my Prince,' called his manservant.

'My father,' he croaked, as loud as he could. 'Send my father here!'

'I think he would rather you came down–'

'Send him here or I'll have you whipped!'

'...Yes, my Prince.'

'Tell him... tell him to come alone.'

The Prince got to his feet and looked in the mirror again. He wasn't dreaming; the snake was still there, watching him with golden eyes that never blinked. Those eyes terrified him. There could be no reasoning with such a creature; it had no compassion, no mercy.

He shuddered as he felt it move slightly. Thankfully, its movement loosened its grip upon his chest, allowing him to breathe more easily.

His door slammed open and the King strode in.

'What is the meaning...'

The King stared at his son.

'What sorcery is this?' said the King.

'I didn't do this,' said the Prince. 'It was the Queen. She gave me a shirt that became a snake.'

'Lies!'

'It's the truth!'

'Lies! Now I know why you are weak and cannot wield a weapon,' said the King, his face twisting into a snarl. 'You have given your mind to magic, and this is what has come of it.

'No sorcerer shall take my throne, nor bring ruin upon my kingdom. Get out. Leave by dark stairs, lest anyone sees you. If they do, I shall have you hunted down and slain like the beast you are.'

The Prince knew his father's mind would not change. He ran past the King and out of the chamber.

Down dark and dusty stairs went the Prince. A hidden escape tunnel led from the cellars to the woods outside the palace. He took it, fleeing into the depths of the forest. Somehow, he could make out the shapes of the trees despite the dark.

The snake weighed heavily on him as he walked, making his back ache. He stopped to rest eventually and sat against a holly tree, the snake's coils pressed between him and the trunk.

What now?

He was no hunter; he couldn't survive in the forest. Yet, if he showed his face in a town or village, he would be driven away or killed. The forest it was, then. He would just have to keep going and hope he found food, or simply starve and die.

He gasped as the snake suddenly tightened its coils around him.

Could it hear his thoughts? What did it want him to do?

'What do you want from me?' he asked.

The snake didn't move, nor loosen its grip.

The Prince sighed. He closed his eyes and tried to rest, but he was too cold. Movement would keep him warm. He got to his feet and kept on walking.

The night seemed to last forever. Owls screeched in the treetops; the murky shapes of forest creatures drew close and then vanished. He stumbled, fell, stood and walked on, until, amid the trees ahead, he saw firelight.

The Prince's heart quickened. He was drawn to the fire, the promise of company; yet he knew there was no hearth where he would be welcome.

He crept forward. The light emanated not from a camp-fire but from the window of a house. Who would build a house here, so deep in the forest?

The Prince drew closer.

Before him stood a tumbledown cottage, with a grass

roof and moss-clad stone walls. He would have thought it long abandoned, but for the light shining through its one tiny window and the smoke rising from the chimney.

Only one kind of person could live here. A witch.

The Prince had never met a witch, and he had no desire to meet one now. Yet only a witch could make sense of what had happened to him, and perhaps cure him.

Summoning his courage, he knocked on the door.

Nothing.

He opened the door and entered the cottage.

The room was warm, the fire heavily-laden. Sitting on a rug by the fire was the witch. A fox lay with its head in her lap.

The Prince expected the fox to leap up and growl at the snake. Instead it lay still, regarding him with calm curiosity, as did the witch. She was so old that she could have been the one who kindled the fires in the stars. Tusks reached from her mouth to her ample belly.

'I'm sorry to bring this serpent into your house,' said the Prince.

'No-one comes here who carries no burden,' said the witch.

She set a pot of broth to heat over the fire. They ate together, and when they had finished, the Prince told his story.

'Can you help me?' he asked.

'No,' said the witch. The Prince's shoulders slumped. 'But I know one who can.

'Do not think yourself saved just yet,' she warned, seeing hope kindle in the Prince's eyes. 'She lives on the Forgotten Island, which lies on a loch near here. She will suffer no man to approach her island, save one.'

'Who?'

'The Ancient Mariner; and he has not picked up an oar since the morning of the world.'

'I must find him.'

'Then go.'

The fox stood, stretched and trotted toward the door. The Prince followed him out into the night.

He followed the fox until morning's first light. As the day awoke, they arrived at the shore of a loch. The loch stretched onto the horizon in both directions. Far out on the water, he could just make out the shape of an island.

Upon the sand was an upturned boat, black with tar. The fox turned and stole away into the forest as the Prince approached the boat.

There was a gap like a door within the boat's stern. The Prince got to his knees and wriggled through. As he did so, the snake's scales bumped against the wood. The Prince winced in pain, as if he had been hit and not the snake.

Inside, he waited as his eyes adjusted to the darkness. Soon, he made out an old grey wolf sitting upon a heap of clothing, and a man lying upon a bed of straw.

The man looked even older than the witch. He was tiny, and starling-thin. His flecked, white skin hung from his bones. Blue veins criss-crossed his body, and he wore not a stitch of clothing.

'I have come looking for the Ancient Mariner,' said the Prince.

'You have found him,' said the Ancient Mariner.

'I wish to cross to the Forgotten Island,' said the Prince.

'I know,' said the Ancient Mariner. 'I have been waiting for you. But I will only go if you can overturn this boat, which no man before you has done.'

The Prince wasn't strong, but he had to try. He wriggled out through the doorway again and slipped his fingers beneath the prow. Tensing his muscles, he heaved and over-turned the boat, sending it crashing down on the sand.

The Ancient Mariner lifted his hand to shield his eyes from the sun.

'You have more strength than you know,' he said. 'Be a good lad and fetch my clothes from under that wolf.'

The Prince walked over to the wolf and tried to push him off the pile of clothes, but the ageing wolf wouldn't move.

'Up!' shouted the Prince. The wolf still wouldn't move, so the Prince kicked him.

'Don't treat him so for warming my trousers,' said the Mariner as the wolf whined and slunk away into the forest.

The Ancient Mariner dressed, and the two of them

pushed the boat into the water. They climbed in, took a set of oars each and set out for the Forgotten Island.

The Prince and the Ancient Mariner rowed all through the day, the snake weighing heavily upon the Prince. At times it tightened its coils, causing him to pull in his oars and gasp for breath. The Mariner would only laugh and strike up a song.

In the afternoon, the Prince looked over his shoulder to see the peaks of the Forgotten Island looming out of the mist. The sight gave him strength, and their boat flew like a cormorant across the water after that.

As they rowed, in a clifftop cave on the Forgotten Island, the witch who ruled the island opened her eyes.

She stood, went to the cave mouth and observed the boat upon the loch. No vessel was permitted to approach the Forgotten Island, and she could have destroyed it with a flick of her hand. Yet the wind carried a song upon it, and she knew the singer's voice. It was the voice of the Ancient Mariner.

The Ancient Mariner and the Prince steered their boat into shore as evening sunlight danced upon the water. Trees lined the shore, stretching towards the mountains at the island's centre.

The Mariner was about to hop from the prow when the witch emerged from the trees.

The Prince and the Mariner watched as she strode to the shore. She moved like water, yet her eyes were full of fire.

'The years have not diminished your beauty, oh–'

'What have you brought here?' the witch asked the Mariner. The sea stirred beneath the boat as she spoke, rocking them from side to side.

'One in need of your help,' he replied.

'There is no help to be found for him here,' she said. 'Turn your boat around.'

The Mariner's shoulders sagged. 'For the sake of what we shared, help the lad.'

'For the sake of what we shared, I am letting you live. Go.'

The Prince and the Mariner turned the boat around and rowed away.

'Halt,' said the Mariner, a little while afterwards. 'Stow your oars.'

The Prince drew in his oars. 'What's wrong–'

The Mariner grabbed hold of the Prince and threw him into the lake.

His lungs full of water, the Prince kicked for the surface. The Mariner was rowing away from him, away from the island.

'Come back!' shouted the Prince, but the Mariner only went on rowing.

The Prince had no choice. He turned and swam for the island, concealed by the dusk.

That night, the Prince shivered miserably on a bed of damp moss. He was angry at the Mariner for deserting him, and at the witch for refusing him help. He was angry at his father for sending him away; at his stepmother for giving him the cursed shirt. Most of all, he was angry at the snake, for all the sorrow it had caused him.

When day came, he walked until he found a meadow, where he lay down to bask in the sun. His stomach gnawed at him like a rat, and he was deathly tired. Save for a few berries, he had found no food.

'Perhaps there are people living on this island, besides the witch,' he said to himself. 'I should go and look for houses and gardens to steal food from.'

The Prince rose and headed inland. His path led him down deer trails and through forests and open meadows, mountains looming ever larger above him.

He wandered all day and saw no dwellings. That night, he slept in a hollow tree.

The Prince wandered on the next day, stopping often to lie down and sleep. Rain fell all day and all night.

On the afternoon of the Prince's fourth day on the island, he spied chimney-smoke in the distance.

His heart skittered in his chest. He was desperate to see people, yet scared of being driven away. No matter; he had to eat. He couldn't go on much longer. The Prince walked with slow, lurching steps now, often stumbling and falling.

He crept as quietly as he could through the forest. The trees thinned out before him. At the forest's edge, he saw the source of the smoke.

Cradled within a green glen was a castle. A river ran by it, and its walls were lined with fish-scales. Deer wandered among lush gardens leading from the castle to the river.

This had to be the home of the witch. If she caught him there, she might kill him. He would have to take that risk.

The Prince stole from shadow to shadow until he stood near the riverbank. Seeing no-one about, he dashed through the shallow water and up the far bank.

He had reached the foot of the castle gardens. Fruit trees surrounded him. He was about to pluck an apple when he saw someone approaching.

It was a maiden. She saw him just as he saw her.

They regarded one another. Her hair and eyes were the deep brown of the otter's coat; she held a peach in her hand.

'Who are you?" she said.

'I was a prince,' he answered. 'Now, I don't know.'

She looked him over, seeing not only the snake but his sunken eyes, soaking clothes and dirt-rimmed fingers.

'You're hungry,' she said. 'Eat something.'

'You're not afraid of me?'

The maiden laughed. 'Why should I be afraid? Here.' She tossed him the peach. He wolfed it down, juices dribbling down his chin. The maiden laughed again, her laughter like the first birdsong of spring. She plucked another peach and fed him that too.

'I should tell my mother that you're here,' said the maiden. Before the Prince could stop her, she turned and ran up the hill towards the castle. The Prince thought about running, but he knew the witch would find him sooner or later, so he waited.

The maiden returned with her mother.

The witch was furious when she saw the Prince. No-one ever dared to defy her. Yet she took in the Prince's sunken eyes, soaking clothes and dirt-rimmed fingers. She saw how he hunched under the weight of the snake. Pity pierced her heart.

'Come inside,' she said. 'You will remain here, until I decide what to do with you.'

The Prince lived in the witch's castle from that day. He was given his own bedchamber and new clothes to wear. The witch's daughter brought his meals to his chamber, for a fever took him shortly after he arrived. As well as meals, she brought him the warmth of her smile, the joy of her company, the reassurance that she cared nothing for the snake coiled about his shoulders. After his fever passed, she led him out for walks in the gardens, the glens and the forests.

The Prince was enamoured with the witch's daughter. She was so different to the girls he knew. Her openness and artlessness were far more beguiling than the false smiles of the women at court. The witch's daughter admired him for not surrendering to the snake's crushing weight. She dreamed of the great man he could be, should he ever be free of it.

The Prince and the witch's daughter fell in love. For the Prince, it was a love that brought no joy in its wake. The serpent's coils smothered any happiness he might have felt.

Eventually, the witch's daughter told her mother that she wished to marry the Prince.

'Do you love him?' asked the witch.

'I do.'

'Would you lose an arm for him?'

'I would.'

'Would you lose a leg for him?'

'I would.'

'Would you lose a breast for him?'

'I would.'

'We shall see,' said the witch.

The witch had three sons. She gathered her sons together one day and said to them, 'Go out and find a wether. Kill it, bring it home and butcher it. Hang the meat up over the kitchen fire.'

Her sons did as she asked. They killed a ram that afternoon and nailed its meat to the wall over the kitchen fire.

Late that night, the witch woke up both her daughter and the Prince. She summoned them to the kitchen, where the fire was burning fiercely in the hearth. Spectral faces appeared and disappeared among the flames.

'You still wish to marry?' she asked them.

'We do,' said her daughter.

'We do,' said the Prince.

'Very well,' said the witch. She gestured to two chairs which stood opposite one another before the fire. 'Sit down.'

They sat and watched the witch as she placed a frying pan on the girdle over the fire.

Next, she took a jar of fat and poured some into the pan. The pan grew hotter, and the fat began to hiss and sizzle.

The Prince felt the snake stir.

'Sit still,' said the witch as the Prince shifted in his seat. 'Don't move or speak unless I say so.'

The witch took a knife in hand. She cut a hunk of meat from the ram's corpse, and dropped it into the pan.

The meat sizzled. Its aroma filled the air.

The snake lunged at the meat.

As soon as it touched the meat, the snake pulled back, burned by the fat. The Prince roared in pain as it writhed, thrashed and jerked, crushing his ribs as it hissed its displeasure.

The witch went to stand behind her daughter.

Reaching down, she took the fabric of her daughter's nightdress between her fingers. She pulled the fabric downwards, revealing the girl's left breast.

The snake fell still. The Prince felt it tense.

Slowly it brought its head forward over his shoulder.

Its tongue flickered.

The snake lunged at the girl's breast. It clasped the breast between its jaws and sank in its fangs.

The girl screamed as the witch raised her knife and brought it down on the snake, severing its head.

The snake's head fell to the floor. Swiftly, the witch set aside her knife and prised the snake's coils from the Prince's back. She threw the body down next to the head, took hold of her biggest pot, upturned it and slammed it down atop them.

Her foot firmly upon the pot, the witch took the knife in hand again. She held it over the fire, turning it three times, muttering spells while her daughter screamed and clutched at her bloody wound.

Still with her foot upon the pot, the witch withdrew the knife from the fire. She wrenched her daughter's hands aside, put the knife to the wound and held it there, sealing the wound closed.

Finally, the witch put aside the knife and lifted the pot. Underneath it was the silken shirt.

She picked up the shirt with the tip of her knife and cast it into the fire. It exploded into black smoke that shrieked, hissed and disappeared.

The snake shirt was gone.

The Prince married the witch's daughter, whose wound quickly healed. A golden breast was forged for her by the island's smith.

Time passed in which the couple spent their every day and night together. The Prince grew accustomed to living without his snake shirt, and his bride grew accustomed to her golden breast. Though it took many weeks, the Prince began to stand up straight, to smile and to laugh. His worries fell away with the autumn leaves.

Autumn gave way to winter. The Prince felt as if he had always lived on the island. He missed the set of pipes he had played as a boy, but apart from that, he had everything he desired.

There was an old washerwoman who came to the castle to wash clothes and scrub floors. She had been a maid to the witch's daughter when the girl was young, and she always took note of what happened in the castle. She knew all about the Prince's snake shirt and his bride's golden breast.

It had always seemed wrong to her that the witch's family lived in a castle while her own family made do with a rundown cottage. For years she had comforted herself with the dream that her son would marry the witch's daughter. She and her son would move into the castle and become part of the family. No longer would she scrub floors on her aching knees.

Though it was only a fantasy, she dreamed it for so long that it took root and grew strong. When the Prince came along and won the girl's heart, she hated him for it. Watching them together in the weeks after their wedding, a plan fermented in her mind.

At home in her cottage, the old woman spoke with her son.

'If I told you,' she said, 'that you could have the witch's daughter for your wife, what would you say?'

'There is no woman whom I would rather marry, Mother,' said her son. 'But she is already married.'

'If you do as I say, she will not be married for long.'

The washerwoman's son sometimes helped out at the castle, hunting for the pot and chopping wood for the fire. One crisp day early in winter, the Prince invited the lad out hunting.

It was the moment the lad had been waiting for.

On their way to the hunting ground, the lad was unusually quiet. He gave short answers to the Prince's questions, and didn't ask any of his own.

'Is something troubling you?' asked the Prince eventually.

'Yes,' said the lad. 'Something is troubling me.'

'Speak it, then.'

The lad halted and turned to face the Prince.

'It's hard for me to say this,' he said, 'but guilt at what I've done is poisoning my mind.'

'What have you done?'

'I have lain with your wife.'

The Prince laughed. It was absurd; he trusted his wife and knew she loved him only. Yet, the lad didn't laugh.

'It's true.'

'Prove it,' said the Prince.

'Your wife,' said the lad, 'has a golden comb.'

The Prince's smile left his lips.

'When you came here, you had a snake wrapped about you.'

The Prince frowned. That was a secret; the witch had allowed no-one to visit the castle while the snake shirt was upon him.

'Your wife,' said the lad, 'has a golden breast.'

With a savage cry, the Prince threw himself at the lad. He

knocked the lad down and pounded him with his fists until he had no breath left in him.

'Get up! Fight me!' said the Prince.

The lad didn't get up. He cowered upon the grass, shielding his face and weeping.

The Prince turned away in disgust. He left the lad lying there and went home to confront his wife.

The Prince's wife was napping on their bed when their chamber door slammed open.

Evening sunlight streamed in through the window, illuminating her husband. He stood at the end of the bed, his face twisted with anger and his fists bloody.

'You lay with the washerwoman's son.'

'What?'

'Admit it. Admit what you did.'

'That's absurd,' she said, rising and reaching for his hands. 'I have not–'

He struck her. Red mist fell like a shroud.

When it lifted, he saw his wife lying on the floor, bloodied and shaking.

'I didn't do this,' he whispered. 'I couldn't...'

The Prince turned and ran from the chamber. Out of the castle doors he ran, down the hill and to the shore. Stealing the first boat he found, the Prince rowed away from the Forgotten Island.

When he reached the far shore, he stripped. Taking the hunting knife from his belt, he hacked at his fine clothes until he resembled a beggar. He cast his fawn-skin boots into the water and walked into the forest.

'The lowest, the most wretched, the worst of men I am,' he said. 'And so I will live.'

Far, far away, and many years later, the Prince sat down at the edge of a marketplace. He hung his head and put out his hand.

Villagers and traders walked past him without giving him a second glance. He was filthy and emaciated, his clothes no more than rags. The nails on his bare toes were yellowed and hardened.

All day, the Prince sat there without a single coin falling into his hand. He was secretly pleased. If he had no coin, he wouldn't eat; if he didn't eat, he would die. He was long past ready to die. Only weakness kept him from death; his fear of hurling himself from a cliff, his inability to refuse his stomach's demands for food.

'Up!' said a voice.

The Prince looked up to see a fat man glaring down at him.

'No beggars allowed in this village after dark. Up you get and clear out, or I'll be back with a whip.'

The Prince got to his feet, his brittle bones complaining at every movement. He walked away from the market and out of the village.

The village lay on the fringe of a kingdom; beyond it was a vast forest. The Prince didn't know if he would find another village within the forest, and he didn't much care. He could steal from farmers' fields if he found any. If he didn't, he would somehow survive, or he would die.

The Prince passed into the forest. In the first few days after leaving the village, he came across a few farms. He helped himself to whatever he could take, before barking dogs sent him fleeing.

He moved deeper into the forest. Roots, tubers, fruits and insects kept him alive.

The worse things were, the happier he was. He had bloodied his fists on his wife's cheek. She had fed him and cared for him, after his own father had turned him away. She had entrusted him with her heart, and he had beat her. He was worse than his stepmother; worse than his father. He was worse than the lad, who might have lain with his wife, or might have tricked him. He deserved all his suffering and more.

The Prince's road led him into a range of mountains. The mountains of the Forgotten Island were but pebbles next to these.

'I will go into the mountains,' said the Prince. 'There will be nothing to eat there, and I will finally die.'

Onwards he went.

A few days later, in a high, stony glen among the mountains, the shivering Prince was trudging down his path when he saw before him a man.

This man was dressed in thick furs. He lay on the ground, motionless.

The Prince knelt down beside him.

'Why are you lying on the ground, up here?' asked the Prince.

'I seek the Spring of Healing,' said the man. 'I thought I was well enough to make it there, but now I am too weak.'

'Where is this spring?' asked the Prince.

'It is not far from here, up among the mountain peaks,' said the man. 'It lies within a cave. It is guarded by an army of animals, who kill anyone who comes seeking its waters. But, at midday, the animals are asleep.'

The Prince looked up at the sky. It was almost midday.

'I will find the spring, and fetch its water for you,' he said.

'Thank you,' said the man. 'You must use the cup. It is guarded by a lion. Take the cup and fill it with water. The water shall cure me of my sickness, and if you drink it, you shall have your heart's desire.'

The Prince left the man. He went on walking until he saw a cave mouth above him.

The Prince began to climb. He reached the cave and entered the gloom.

The cave was enormous. Spear-shafts of midday sunlight pierced the darkness, illuminating the guardians of the cave.

Within the cave were all the fierce animals of the world. Bears and leopards, wolves and stoats, foxes and vipers lay down side by side upon the dusty stones.

The Prince crept among them. Every animal slept; but for how long? He couldn't risk stepping on a paw or tail. Slowly and silently, he moved deeper into the cave.

In the far, deep belly of the cave, the Prince found the spring.

It lay at the centre of a circular cavern. A pillar of sunlight streaming from a gap in the ceiling above, illuminating its crystalline waters.

Surrounding it was a pride of a lions.

The lionesses lay close to another, their cubs nestled in beside them. Closest to the spring was a golden-maned lion.

Ever so carefully, the Prince stepped between the lionesses until he reached the lion.

Beneath one of its forepaws was a two-handled golden cup.

The lion's chest rose and fell with its breath, slivers of steam rising from its jaws. It slept with its eyes open, just a fraction.

All he had to do was reach out and take the cup. If the lion awoke and killed him, so be it. If it didn't, the sick man would be healed, and he would have his heart's desire.

For all that, the Prince found himself unable to move.

Leave, said a voice in his mind. *Climb higher into the mountains. Let the cold take you. It will all be over.*

The Prince turned away from the lion.

In his mind's eye, he saw his bride. The way she had looked at him, that first day in the garden. Her bloodied face, the day he beat her.

He turned around and knelt down.

He looked into the slits of the lion's eyes.

The Prince took the cup from under the lion's paw.

The lion growled and stood up. It yawned and walked away from the Prince, out of the cave. The lionesses and cubs followed it.

The Prince filled the cup. He walked back through caves that were now deserted. The hunting beasts had gone.

The Prince found the sick man lying where he had left him. He gave the man half of the water in the cup, and the man was healed.

When the man had finished drinking, the Prince took the cup and put it to his lips.

He was back on the Forgotten Island.

His clothes were mended. He wore boots upon his feet. In his arms was a set of bagpipes, just like the ones he had played as a boy.

The Prince crossed the island until he stood outside of the castle. Beneath the starry sky, he put the chanter to his lips and began to play.

Within the castle, his wife awoke.

She heard the music he played. It was both fierce and gentle, like the eagle's song. It reminded her of him.

She went to her window. Her husband stood in the place where they had first met, playing a set of pipes.

The Prince's wife left her chamber and knocked on her eldest brother's door.

'What would you do,' she asked him, 'if I told you my husband was outside?'

'I would break his jaw for beating you and the lad,' said her eldest brother.

She went to her next eldest brother's chamber.

'What would you do,' she asked him, 'if I told you my husband was outside?'

'Break his bones and cast him from the roof,' said her brother, 'for beating you and the lad, and for accusing you of shaming him.'

She went to her youngest brother's chamber.

'What would you do,' she asked, 'if I told you my husband was outside?'

'I would welcome him,' said her youngest brother. 'For if

he is outside, he is the one playing those pipes; and in his music, I hear his true heart.'

'He is outside.'

Downstairs and out of the castle doors she went. When her husband saw her, he put down his pipes and they embraced. She forgave him for what he had done, and in time, her mother and brothers did too. They passed away long ago, and from that night, their hearts never knew sorrow.[1]

---

1. *I heard this story from Donald Smith many years ago and was utterly enchanted. Afterwards, I bought the book he found it in,* The Summer Walkers *by Timothy Neat, a study of Traveller culture. I read it as an initiation story, depicting a young man's struggle to accept and integrate his shadow side. Look out for a future book exploring this story in depth.*

AUTHOR'S NOTE

I hope you enjoyed reading these stories. Though I know most of them very well, I got to know them better by writing this collection. I'm very grateful for that.

Choosing which stories to include wasn't easy. I wanted to be representative of the entire country while covering all the most prominent mythical creatures. But there were just too many amazing stories; too many weird and wonderful creatures. If you were expecting brownies, blue men, the Wulver or Scathach... hang on for Volume II. I'll get to it soon.

You might be wondering to what extent I adapted the stories. The debate among storytellers about how much one can change a story will never end, nor should it. It's an important question. I generally go with the rule that you can add a flavour here and there, but you can't change the recipe.

Being a novelist as well as a storyteller, I tend to enjoy adding in some extra detail when writing down oral stories. I try to flesh out characters without weighing them down, which can be tricky. There's a reason why it's usually 'the Prince' or 'the girl' rather than a named character. The inhabitants of the stories don't occupy the same reality as us; they're closer to symbols or archetypes than skin-and-bone people. If I say 'the Prince', that could be me as much as it could be you. If I say 'Betty', it happened to Betty.

What next?

If any of these stories captured your heart, I'd highly recommend seeking them out in other guises. Better than that, memorise the essentials of your favourite story and tell it yourself. Write it out, draw it, dance it, tell it to a llama. You'll see new sides to the story, just as you learn new things about your best friend by taking them out somewhere new.

When you're ready, tell your story to some two-legged people. Magical things happen when you clear your throat and unlock your word-hoard; and all that's needed is a teller, a listener and a tale. There's no fancy equipment required. It's a radical and rebellious thing.

If you liked my way of telling the stories, you'd probably enjoy my other books too. I have a novel, *The Shattering Sea*. It's set in Iron Age Orkney and is based on the tale of *Asipattle and the Maester Stoor Worm*. If fast-paced fantasy stories that twist and turn like a viper are your thing, you should probably buy a copy.

I have another book completed but not available to buy yet. *Finn & the Fianna* is a retelling of the Fianna stories, from Finn's birth to the breaking of the Fianna. It includes my favourite of all tales, *Diarmuid & Grainne*. You can learn more about it on my website.

This book is the first volume of my *Celtic Myths & Legends Retold* series. The next book will focus on the Irish hero Cuchulainn, who trained with the witch queen Scathach on Skye.

I have a weekly podcast, House of Legends, on which myself and some of the world's best storytellers tell the myths, legends and folktales that we love. I'd love it if you subscribed, which you can do on any podcast app.

If you'd like a bit of help with telling stories, I run an online coaching group for storytellers called Myth Singers. You can find out more on my website.

If you want to write your first novel – and are absolutely, totally committed to doing so – you can get in touch with me about book coaching.

I have a readers' club called The House of Legends Clan. By joining, you'll be the first to get news on my podcast, books, blog posts, coaching groups, retreats and live events, as well as exclusive discount offers. You can unsubscribe at any time, and it's quick and easy to do so. As soon as you join, you'll get my free ebook, *Silverborn & Other Tales*. Find out more on my website.

Feel free to email me to tell me which stores you loved. I'd love to hear from you. And please do leave a review. They help me and they help other readers.

Lastly, why not do some digging under your own cabbage patch? I bet there are loads of amazing stories waiting for you there. I'd love to hear them.

Daniel Allison

FREE DOWNLOAD OFFER

As the winter winds shriek and their family sleeps, Grunna and Talorc sit at the hearth-fire, telling the tales of Ancient Orka. Stories of trowies, silkies and even the mysterious Silvers.

I'm offering *Silverborn* as a FREE ebook exclusively to members of The House of Legends Clan. Visit my website to collect and download. It's fast, free and easy.

Get my FREE ebook at www.houseoflegends.me/landing-page

There follows a sample chapter of
The Bone Flute
by Daniel Allison

THE SHATTERING SEA (SAMPLE CHAPTER)

ORKNEY, CIRCA 500BC

Talorc crawled through the forest of dune-grass, listening to the stranger sing. He couldn't see the singer yet, but it had to be a stranger. No-one he knew would steal out before dawn to sing up the sun, except Grunna, and she was dead.

The wind was fierce this morning, its howling covering the sound of his approach. Talorc wanted to see the stranger, but he didn't want the stranger to see him. Why not? Because this was Odhran, and no-one ever came here except in Grunna's stories, about marauders from the sea who stole away women and murdered men, or about finmen who came ashore at night to perform their secret spells.

Talorc reached the dune's peak and looked down.

Moonlight silvered the sand. Upon the sand stood the stranger. He wore a sealskin cloak and faced away from

Talorc, north towards the sea, his arms spread wide as if he wished all the sea-creatures and the hidden stars to listen. His voice was deep and grating and his words made no sense. At his side was a skin-sack, and beside it a heap of seagrass.

The sack was moving.

Talorc noticed this but didn't dwell on it. Faint voices whispered in his mind as his gaze fixed on the scaled, blue-black skin on the stranger's hands, on his bare feet and on the coiled tail resting between his legs on the sand.

Talorc knew that he knew almost nothing of the world. He knew his village, half a mile south-east of the beach. He knew the beach, and the western cliffs where seabirds nested, and the rolling hills to the south and their scattered farmsteads. Not once had been to the south of the island, nor to any other island in Orka, nor out to sea. But he knew Orka's stories. He knew about finmen.

This was a finman.

The sack moved again. Something was alive inside it. The finman went on singing as he kicked it with the heel of his foot.

Whatever was inside the sack whined and fell still.

The finman ceased his rasping song. He walked around the sack, the hood of his cloak obscuring his face, and knelt over the mound of seagrass. Talorc watched as his long, scaled fingers arranged it into the shape of an arrow, complete with flight-feathers and barbed point. The arrow faced south-east, towards Talorc. Towards the village.

The sky was brightening. Talorc's family would be awake now and at the harvesting soon. He would be in for another skelping.

The finman now went to the sack. Was it really a finman? They were forbidden to leave their island, except to fish in the waters around it. Sometimes folk said they had seen one out at sea, but only ever for a few moments, and there was never any proof. But only finmen had tails, and blue-black glittering scales. It had to be a finman, which meant that this was the most exciting thing that had ever happened to Talorc. He had a story of his own to tell now. It also meant that he was in danger, for the finman was breaking the treaty, and if he knew Talorc was there...

Talorc's thoughts were interrupted as the finman pulled from the sack a fat seal pup. He held it aloft as it struggled, wriggling as it keened for its mother in sharp yelps. The finman let it struggle while he resumed his song. Though Talorc didn't understand his words, there was a feeling of finality to them, like the way Grunna had spoken when nearing the end of a story, or the way she had played the last few notes of a tune on her bone-flute. The white-furred, black-eyed pup seemed to sense it too and writhed more desperately, keened more loudly.

The finman lowered the pup to his chest, out of Talorc's sight.

Day had come. The sand shifted from silver to white in

the faint approaching sunlight. The wind howled like a bone-flute played by a giant in the sky.

The finman reached into his skin-cloak, withdrew a stone knife and held it up high. Talorc's heart pounded as if trying to break free.

The finman's song reached its peak. The final note resounded.

The knife flashed down. Flashed up again.

Red blood poured from the pup onto the arrow as Talorc screamed.

The finman turned and looked straight at him.

THE SHATTERING SEA: BOOK I OF THE ORKNEY CYCLE

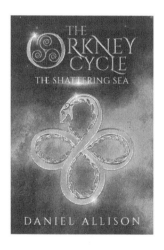

In Iron Age Orkney, two races stand on the brink of war.

The finfolk have summoned an Azawan, a creature of nightmare, and the Orkadi are powerless to stop it. Runa,

Princess of the Orkadi, and Talorc, whose family were slain by demon, come together to destroy it.

The truths they uncover will change their world forever – if they live long enough to share them.

'A tremendous read... no end of dramas, surprises & reversals of fortune... a rattling good plot... wonderful stuff'
Fay Sampson, Guardian Children's Book Award-Nominated Author

'A born storyteller weaves Scottish island myths into a driving narrative of survival'
Ian Stephen, Saltire Award-Nominated Author

AVAILABLE NOW FROM HOUSE OF LEGENDS PRESS
WWW.HOUSEOFLEGENDS.ME

FINN & THE FIANNA
AVAILABLE SOON FROM THE HISTORY PRESS

The stories of Finn MacCoul and his warriors were once told at every fireside in Scotland and Ireland. After centuries in obscurity, this collection brings the tales soaring to life again.

Within these pages are Diarmuid, whom no woman can help but love, and Ossian, a warrior-poet raised in the woods by a wild deer. There is Grainne, ancient ancestor of Iseult and Guinevere; and Finn himself, whose name was once a byword for wisdom, generosity and beauty.

Enter a world of feasting and fighting, battles and poetry, riddles and omens; join Finn and the Fianna on their never-ending quest to drink deeper and deeper of the cup of life.

'A masterpiece... this is Celtic myths and legends at their fantastic best! Your eyes dare not blink for fear of missing a single word. Mythical, flirty, thumpingly violent and divinely nasty!'

Jess Smith, Author of *Way of the Wanderers*

RECOMMENDED READING

There are many books on Scottish folklore; these are some of my personal favourites.

Breslin, Theresa & Leiper, Kate, 'An Illustrated Treasury of Scottish Folk & Fairy Tales' (Floris, 2012)

Bruford, Alan & Macdonald, Donald, 'Scottish Traditional Tales' (Birlinn, 2018)

Campbell, David, 'Out of the Mouth of the Morning' (Luath, 2009)

Campbell, John Francis, 'Popular Tales of the West Highlands Volumes I-IV' (Amazon Media)

Campbell, John Gregorson, 'Waifs and Strays of CelticTradition Vol. IV' (Leopold, 2016) & 'The Gaelic Otherworld' (Birlinn, 2019)

Mackenzie, Donald, 'Wonder Tales from Scottish Myth & Legend' (Forgotten Books, 2016)

Montgomery, Norah, 'The Fantastical Feats of Finn MacCoul' (Birlinn, 2009)

Montgomery, Norah & William, 'The Folk Tales of Scotland; The Well at World's End and Other Stories' (Birlinn, 2008)

Muir, Tom, 'Orkney Folk Tales' (The History Press, 2014) & 'The Mermaid Bride' (Orcadian Ltd, 2008)

Nagy, Joseph, 'The Wisdom of the Outlaw: The Boyhood Deeds of Finn in Gaelic Narrative Tradition' (University of California Press, 1985)

Patterson, Rachel, 'Pagan Portals; The Cailleach' (Moon Books, 2016)

Stephen, Ian, 'Western Isles Folk Tales' (History Press, 2018)

Williamson, Duncan, 'Flight of The Golden Bird'

HOUSE OF LEGENDS PODCAST

If you loved this book, you'll love House of Legends. It's a podcast on which I tell my favourite myths and legends; the kind of dark, weird and brilliant stories that inspired me to write this book. I also use the podcast to keep readers up to date with what I'm working on and my upcoming live events.

'The most soothing voice in podcasting'
Wine & Crime Podcast

'The best mythology podcast I've heard'
Listener Review

'Relaxing, engaging and pure talent'
The History of Vikings Podcast

You can subscribe at Apple Podcasts, Spotify, Stitcher or any good podcast app. You can also listen on my website.

STORYTELLING COACHING

I offer online coaching for new and intermediate storytellers. Whether you want tell on stage or have your children begging for a bedtime story, my Myth Singers coaching groups will give you the skills you need.

'As early as the first session, Daniel laid out a framework for us to follow and gave us fun and creative techniques to play with. It's been really inspiring. During the online meet ups we all take turns to share our stories, and we receive constructive feedback on how to develop both the tale and the delivery further. I'm really excited to see what unfolds!'

— JEMIMA TAYLOR

BOOK COACHING
FROM FIRST THOUGHTS TO FINAL DRAFT

Are you ready to write your first novel? If the answer is yes, and you are seriously committed to making your dream a reality, I would like to offer you book coaching. Whether you have an idea or a first draft, I can provide you with support, feedback and accountability to help see you through to the finish line.

Contact me for details.

ACKNOWLEDGMENTS

This book wouldn't have been written were it not for Donald Smith and his tireless work to champion the Scottish story-telling tradition. To Donald, Annalisa, Daniel and everyone at the Scottish Storytelling Centre, thank you for all the work you do.

To David Campbell, thank you for bringing these stories alive for me and for living the spirit of the Fianna every day.

Thank you to all my friends in the storytelling world for sharing the journey: Fiona, Claire, Wajuppa, Mona, Ruth, Liz, Kamini, David, Dougie, Janis, Tom, Ian, Ana, Martina, Maria, Angharad, Eric, Suzanne, Amy, Mara, Marion, Stina, Michael, Mio, Ray, Beverley, Joshua and everyone else keeping their traditions alive.

Jake, Fiona, Lindsay, Jane, Beverley, thank you for your eagle eyes.

To Martin Shaw and Ken Shapley, thank you for lighting this fire.

Sean, Liz and my Muay Thai family, thank you for the motivation to always keep moving forward and never stay down.

Sheila, thank you for being such a pleasure to work with.

Mum, Peter, Paul, Rachel, Maia, thank you for your support in everything.

Florence and Mimi, thank you for keeping my desk warm. Please stop fighting.

ABOUT THE AUTHOR

Daniel Allison is an author, oral storyteller, podcaster and coach from Scotland. He is the author of *The Shattering Sea*, *Silverborn & Other Tales*, *Scottish Myths & Legends* and *Finn & The Fianna*. Daniel has lived in India, Nepal, Uganda and Thailand, and now divides his time between Scotland and Thailand. His work explores the meeting places of myth, history, literature and ritual. He loves cats and hates celery.

You can keep up to date with Daniel by subscribing to his podcast, by writing to him or by joining the House of Legends Clan.

Printed in Great Britain
by Amazon